W9-AVS-892

"Oh—wait! Please!"

Noah's plan to make a swift exit was thwarted by his hostess's entreaty. When he turned, she was lumbering down the stairs, a protective hand on her stomach. Her descent was precariously rapid and he automatically headed in her direction.

"Don't—you'll fall." He jogged up several steps and took her arm. "What's so important?"

"You—can't go!" Sally said, short of breath. "What do I tell them?"

Noah was confused. "About what?"

"About us—being deliriously happy!"

"I don't care what you tell them." He separated her desperate, clutching fingers from his shirtfront and took off the wedding ring she'd given him. "Tell your grandparents whatever you want. Have a good life."

She made a pained face. "I'll pay you!"

"I don't want your money."

"What do you want? I'll do anything!" she cried.

What happens when you suddenly discover your happy twosome is about to be turned into a...*family?*

Do you panic?
Do you laugh?
Do you cry?
Or...do you get married?

The answer is all of the above—and plenty more!

Share the laughter and the tears as these unsuspecting couples are plunged into parenthood!

READY FOR BABY

When parenthood takes you by surprise!

HER HIRED HUSBAND

Renee Roszel

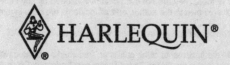

TORONTO • NEW YORK • LONDON
AMSTERDAM • PARIS • SYDNEY • HAMBURG
STOCKHOLM • ATHENS • TOKYO • MILAN • MADRID
PRAGUE • WARSAW • BUDAPEST • AUCKLAND

If you purchased this book without a cover you should be aware
that this book is stolen property. It was reported as "unsold and
destroyed" to the publisher, and neither the author nor the
publisher has received any payment for this "stripped book."

To my sons, Doug and Randy.
Little did I know the eighteen months I spent pregnant
with you guys would turn out to be the hardest,
yet most rewarding research I've ever done!
Love, Mom

ISBN 0-373-03682-5

HER HIRED HUSBAND

First North American Publication 2001.

Copyright © 2001 by Renee Roszel Wilson.

All rights reserved. Except for use in any review, the reproduction or
utilization of this work in whole or in part in any form by any electronic,
mechanical or other means, now known or hereafter invented, including
xerography, photocopying and recording, or in any information storage
or retrieval system, is forbidden without the written permission of the
publisher, Harlequin Enterprises Limited, 225 Duncan Mill Road,
Don Mills, Ontario, Canada M3B 3K9.

All characters in this book have no existence outside the imagination of
the author and have no relation whatsoever to anyone bearing the same
name or names. They are not even distantly inspired by any individual
known or unknown to the author, and all incidents are pure invention.

This edition published by arrangement with Harlequin Books S.A.

® and TM are trademarks of the publisher. Trademarks indicated with
® are registered in the United States Patent and Trademark Office, the
Canadian Trade Marks Office and in other countries.

Visit us at www.eHarlequin.com

Printed in U.S.A.

CHAPTER ONE

SALLY forced a smile as she stared at the two people she disliked most in the world. What a shame they were nearly all the family she had. In her head, she knew she didn't owe them any explanations, but her heart told her to lie.

The sound of a car crunching over the gravel driveway alerted her to the fact that her fake husband had arrived. Exhaling with relief, she blessed her brother for coming through for her. "Excuse me—grandmother, grandfather." She rushed out of the parlor to her front door.

Well, "rushed" might not be the best word, since she was eight months pregnant, and at the moment rushing wasn't something she did with great skill. Her heart thudded as she flung open the door and tramped down the plank stairs, clutching the worn wood rail with one hand. The other was unconsciously spread across her belly, a protective gesture. "Thank goodness," she mumbled, a little winded. She checked her watch. "Perfect timing."

The man who emerged from the pickup truck was better looking than she'd hoped for. Several inches over six feet tall, he made a striking presence in a beige polo shirt, khaki trousers and Roper boots. Wide shoulders didn't hurt the tall-dark-and-handsome look one bit. Black, neatly trimmed hair glistened like Texas crude oil in the mild, early March sunshine. Her gaze was drawn to his eyes—amazing, mirror-bright blue, of the heavy-lidded, bedroom variety. With lashes that swept out like summertime awnings. Gazing into those eyes struck a long-dormant chord and she experienced a twinge of desire. *Fine timing,* she admonished inwardly. *To him you look like the Goodyear Blimp!*

Leave it to Sam to recruit the best-looking orderly at the hospital. She'd worried about what pitiful specimen of mankind would agree to her ploy and actually show up. She was pleasantly shocked by this guy. Of course, considering Sam's renowned bedside manner, her doctor-brother could talk a duck into an oven if he put his mind to it.

She hadn't realized she'd smiled at that thought until the man smiled back. The pleasant expression was a slight, one-sided job. Even so, with those great male lips, that lopsided grin did more to her than most full-fledged grins. She actually tingled with appreciation. *Stop it, ninny,* she scolded herself mentally. *Don't get giddy and feminine. Time's wasting! He's doing you a favor, now get on with it!*

Her boldly handsome orderly rounded the truck and held out a hand. "Hi, Sam sent me to—"

"I know." She grabbed his outstretched fingers and tugged him up the wooden steps. "Follow my lead." She hauled him through the door. "Oh—and you're a *doctor.*" Her whisper held an urgent, life-or-death edge.

Just before entering the parlor, she remembered the ring. *"Darn!"* Skidding to a halt, she fished around in her smock pocket, grabbed it and shoved it onto his finger. By some miracle, it fit. "That was close." She cast him a quick, conspiratorial look.

His eyes had narrowed slightly and he stared at her curiously. She made a sheepish face. "It's more traditional." She grasped the hand she'd slipped the wedding band on and slung it over her shoulder. "Now, *please, smile!*" she commanded under her breath. "We're deliriously happy!"

She skimmed an arm around his waist. This whole farce with her grandparents was traumatic, and awkward in the extreme, but it didn't diminish her ability to detect how solid he felt, how nice he smelled. Determinedly she drew him into the parlor, a homey disorder of overstuffed and slightly frayed furniture in a kaleidoscope of bright patterns. Until she witnessed the undisguised repulsion in her grandparents' eyes the place had never seemed shabby or garish. Now, she looked around, unnerved.

She felt a tightening in her belly and knew it wasn't her baby daughter kicking, but regret and hostility. *How dare they make her feel inferior without even a word!* That was why they were here, wasn't it—to look down their Boston blue-blooded noses on their inadequate and tainted granddaughter?

With a quick shake of her head, she stuffed her anger and got herself on track. "Honey, I want you to meet my grandparents. Abigail and Hubert Vanderkellen, from Boston." She slanted the best grin she could manage toward her fake-devoted-husband, not quite able to look him in those gorgeous blue eyes. "Remember? I told you they'd drop by for a quick visit before leaving on their cruise later today?"

The orderly glanced at her when she spoke. His inspection shifted to the older couple, sitting stiffly on the red-and-yellow floral sofa. Several heartbeats went by as he stared at them. Sally wondered what was going through his mind. He almost looked as if he was seeing a ghost. Weird.

A second later he returned his gaze to her face, his brows knitting. She experienced a rush of panic and pinched him above his belt. Those stunning eyes sharpened. She didn't blame him for being annoyed by the nip of her fingers, but hadn't Sam explained this was important? She wouldn't lie about being married if it weren't absolutely necessary.

She faked a giggle and focused on her grandparents. "My—sweetie is a wonderful doctor, but he's a little forgetful." She glanced back at the tall man beside her. She smiled, but shot a desperate plea with her eyes, begging him to get into the script and *now*. "Grandmother and grandfather, I'd like you to officially meet my husband—Dr. Thomas…Step. "

Step? She flinched. That name came out of nowhere. How lame! Couldn't she have thought of something more substantial? Even if she stuck to the ridiculous staircase theme, at least Banister? She tried to squelch her annoyance. It was simply bad luck she'd been looking at the stairs in the mirror over the fireplace. What difference did it make what name she made up, anyway? In an hour her grandparents would be gone.

"How do you do?" Abigail Vanderkellen said, her hands remaining clasped in her lap. "I suppose I can understand why neither Sam nor Sally told us of her marriage." She flicked a reproving glance at her granddaughter. "There has been a bit of a strain in our relationship."

A bit? Sally scoffed behind her forced smile. *Like the sinking of the Titanic was a bit of bad luck!*

Abigail Vanderkellen shifted to present her stern look at the orderly. "Of course, you know all about that. Tom, is it?"

He cleared his throat, and Sally had a bad feeling. She shot him a terrified glance, but too late. She only caught the snap of his eyes as he looked away. She would have given anything to know what he was thinking.

"Actually, no."

He lifted his hand from her shoulder, and Sally could only watch helplessly as he walked around the rough-hewn pine coffee table. Her heart leaped up to lodge in her throat, cutting off her ability to breathe. *Actually, no?* What did he think he was he doing?

"I can say with all honesty she's told me nothing about your relationship." He extended a hand toward Abigail. "And my friends call me Noah." He continued to hold his position until the older woman unclenched her fists and belatedly accepted his hand. After their brief contact, he turned to Hubert. "Thomas Noah Step," he said, shaking the older man's hand.

Sally's heart hammered so deafeningly in her ears, she wasn't sure she heard right. *Thomas Noah Step?* Then— then he was going along with it, after all. Thank goodness!

Hubert gave Noah a look. "You look somewhat familiar, young man."

"I can't say I'm surprised. I have one of those faces." The orderly said, wearing an odd half grin. "Had we ever met, Mr. Vanderkellen, I'm sure I would remember you." His gaze shifted to Mrs. Vanderkellen. "Both."

Harboring enough misgiving to choke a horse, Sally watched her fake husband retrace his steps. This guy may have agreed to be a part of her scheme, but he didn't follow orders well. What was that unnecessary insistence on being Noah? Why couldn't he have gone with Tom and saved her a near heart attack?

To her astonishment, he replaced his arm across her shoulder, even giving her an affectionate squeeze. "I'd forgotten you two were dropping by." He turned to Sally. "Darling, how long did you say they'd be here?"

"Uh—an hour."

He glanced at his watch. "Ah."

Ah? What did that mean? Didn't Sam give this guy *any* of the details? Why the frown at his watch? Did he have a train to catch? From looking at him, it was more likely a hot date.

"Is there a problem, Dr. Step?" Hubert asked.

Noah faced the older man and smiled. "Noah. And no. No problem." He looked down at Sally. "Why don't you sit, sweetheart?" He aimed her toward an overstuffed chair and ottoman, liberally splashed with daffodils. "Elevate your feet. You know how your ankles swell when you stand."

Reflexively she checked her ankles. They weren't swollen. They'd never been swollen a day in her pregnancy. She gave him a look that wasn't totally loving. "My ankles are fine—*honey.*"

He grinned, this time the act involved his whole mouth and some dazzling teeth. She sat down heavily, more out of a mysterious weakness in the knees than an excess of water on her ankles. She had to give this My-

Friends-Call-Me-Noah credit. He had a way with smiling.

She watched him in a state of agitated awe as he moved to take a seat on the sofa with her priggish grandparents. *Don't say anything that'll blow it for me!* she silently threw out, hoping he was better at telepathy than blind obedience. He was acting like the lord of the manor!

"So…" Noah extended an arm along the back of the couch, looking relaxed and in charge. "You're Sally's grandparents. On her mother's side?"

Both Hubert and Abigail shifted in unison and stared, looking shocked. "Well, of course!" Abigail said, affront edging her tone. "Surely you knew that!"

"Not necessarily." He turned on that whopping big, sexy grin again. "Look at her. Does it look like we did much talking?"

Sally could not believe that lewd remark. Her cheeks sizzled and maintaining her smile became the hardest work she'd ever done. Her baby kicked and she placed her hands over her belly. Apparently she wasn't the only female in the room affected by his smile.

"H-honey," she said, trying to pretend amusement. "Please."

His wink was alarmingly wicked. "Sorry, sweetheart, but you know how you affect me." He turned back to the open-mouthed Vanderkellens. "So, you're from Boston," he went on, conversationally.

With his direct observation, Abigail and Hubert recaptured their poise and even seemed to swell a bit. Being Vanderkellens from Boston was no small thing.

Everybody who was anybody in Boston knew Abigail and Hubert Vanderkellen.

"Why, yes, we are," Hubert said, though he didn't smile.

Sally watched them preen.

"Have you ever been there?" Abigail asked, toying theatrically with a diamond earring, her knobby fingers heavy with all manner of pretentious stones.

"I don't mean to brag, but the Vanderkellens are an old, old family," Hubert added, making a production of fluffing a loosely folded maroon pocket square.

"I don't get up north much," Noah said.

"What a shame." Abigail looked truly sorry for him. "Boston is one of America's great, historical cities."

"Houston's got a little history, too," he said.

"I'm sure." Abigail's tone was so haughty, she might as well have said, "Don't be ridiculous."

Sally ran a hand through her hair, wishing the time would pass more quickly. The clock on the brick mantel had only traveled fifteen minutes since her handsome partner in crime had arrived. She scanned her grandparents, willing them to disappear.

Her antagonism bubbled to the surface. Stuffy and snobbish and narrow-minded, they sat, looking as though they feared the old farmhouse that had been her family's home, teemed with rats and roaches and all manner of vermin that might thrive in such an uncouth wilderness.

Abigail touched as little of the sofa as possible, obviously trying not to contaminate her precious, cream-colored cashmere suit. Hubert didn't appear much more comfortable about the safety of his brass-buttoned, navy Prince of Wales blazer and gray slacks. He crossed his legs and bumped the coffee table with a foot, drawing Sally's attention to hand-sewn leather wing tips.

When he pulled a white handkerchief from an inside pocket and wiped the leather as though contact with her table had streaked it with grime, she had to struggle to keep from screaming. So what if his darn shoes cost more than all the furniture in her parlor? Her home might be a little cluttered, but it was *not* dirty!

Both Abigail and Hubert patted their hair at the same time, a bizarre mutuality, as though they shared one brain. Both had perfectly coiffed silver locks—Abigail's caplike hairdo not quite as long or thick or bouffant as Hubert's. Since they hadn't been part of Sally's life, she didn't know if they'd looked so much alike some fifty-odd years ago when they were married.

Right now, they were equally hawk-nosed and pinch-eyed. Only their mouths were noticeably different. Hubert had a little slice of a mouth and no discernible lips. Abigail's lips were wide, and eternally turned down disapprovingly at the corners. They would have been like her mother's, except for the arrogance they broadcast.

They were dressed for Boston's chilly March weather, not Houston's balmy warmth. They had to be dying of the heat, but were too cultured to show it. Besides, they would never allow themselves to acknowledge Texas existed—except in the bad dream where their headstrong daughter ran off to marry beneath her.

"Sometime when you're here longer, we'll give you a tour."

Sally flicked her glance to her lounging fake-mate. What did he think he was doing?

"Excuse me?" Hubert asked.

"A tour—of Houston," Noah repeated, with a casual host-of-the-manor smile. "We'd love to, wouldn't we, sweetheart?"

Their eyes met. His twinkled. *Twinkled!* He seemed to be having fun playing the part of her deliriously happy husband. But to make such sweeping statements about taking her grandparents on a tour of Houston? That was going way over the line. She might be paying him fifty bucks for this performance, but she didn't intend to put him on the payroll forever.

The last thing on earth she wanted was to spend more than an hour with these insufferable people. She aimed a hard-fought smile at him and nodded, unable to trust her voice.

"You know what?" Noah said, sitting forward.

Sally had no idea, and she wasn't sure she wanted to find out. She swallowed.

"What we need is something cool to drink." He stood. "Honey?"

"Oh—there's tea in the fridge." She started to get up, but he moved to her side, pressing down on her shoulder. "Don't trouble yourself, sweetheart." He bent and kissed her, his lips warm and lazily seductive. The contact was brief, but the effect was dizzying. Light-headed and short of breath, she could feel a slow, tingling sensation spread outward along her limbs.

"Your ankles, remember?" His lips quirked with mild amusement. Luckily his head blocked her face from her grandparents' view, since her expression was probably shell-shocked. Her cheeks burned, a distinct sign she was blushing. "Point me toward the kitchen," he whispered.

The request sounded like so much static at first, but belatedly his meaning sank in and she canted her head slightly to her left. He straightened, calling over his shoulder. "Who takes sugar?"

"I do," Sally said, then bit her tongue. *A husband would know that, dummy!*

His chuckle echoed around the room. "As if I could forget."

"I don't think we have time for tea," Hubert called.

"Sure you do," Noah said. "I'll only be a minute."

Sally hadn't realized until after he'd left that simply having him there, master-of-the-house persona or no, was a big help. So far, he'd commanded most of the conversation. She cleared her throat and knotted her hands on her belly. "So—where are you going on your cruise?"

"The first week will include a walking tour of the pyramids of Cozumel, after that, the usual Caribbean stops."

"Oh…" Sally didn't know what to say. She knew about as much about Cozumel pyramids as she did about Mars. Once again, she felt like the inadequate Johnson sibling. Her big brother, Sam, was a doctor. She'd dropped out of college after one semester, to concentrate on her metal sculpture.

Sam had visited Boston once, last year. He'd laughingly told her their grandparents referred to her as "a welder," and in a whisper, on the rare occasions they mentioned her mortifying status at all. Good old Sam thought their stuffy Victorianism was hilarious, and cast it off as unimportant. But she hadn't. Every time she thought about it, the mental picture pecked new holes in her self-esteem. She could just see them grasping at their hearts and gasping, "A Vanderkellen—*welding!*" It was unthinkable.

"I understand Sam is leaving this afternoon on vacation, too," Abigail said, drawing Sally from her morose thoughts. She nodded. "Scuba diving in—Bon—Bon—" She couldn't remember.

"Bonaire," came a deep, male voice.

She turned in time to see Noah stroll in, four tall glasses on a wicker tray.

"H-how did you know?" she asked, then cringed. If she wasn't careful she'd blow this herself. After all, he did know Sam. Evidently he'd heard her brother discussing it. She blew out a breath. There was his explanation. Simple and not even a lie.

"Don't you remember, darling?" He glanced at her as he lay the tray on the coffee table. "You told me about Bonaire this morning while we were in the shower."

She realized her lips had dropped open in a shocked "oh" and clamped her jaws. *In the shower?* Had he actually said *in the shower?*

She cast a worried glance at her grandparents. Abigail's eyes were a fraction wider and Hubert tugged at his collar.

Her gaze zapped back to Noah, bending over the tray. If she stretched, she could just about kick that taut backside. He probably thought he was the funniest orderly at the hospital.

Opting not to get physical, she cleared her throat meaningfully, but he didn't seem to notice as he handed two glasses to her grandparents. A flash of orange and black told her he'd found some paper napkins. Unfortunately they were covered with Halloween witches and pumpkins. Well, they'd been cheap at the day-after-Halloween sale, and they worked just fine. She must not let herself feel like an inferior hostess for being frugal.

When Noah handed her a glass, he said, "Six teaspoons of sugar, right, honey?"

She smiled thinly. "Perfect." She was going to die of sugar toxicity, but the show must go on. As he ambled around to seat himself on the couch, he winked at her, blatantly flaunting their illicit collaboration. She sucked in a startled breath. What if her grandparents had seen him?

Though she was highly annoyed at his audacity, and promised herself she'd strangle him the first chance she had, she couldn't stifle a wry giggle. Not only had his wink been unsubtle, but it had been sexy and appealing. Trying to adjust her attitude, she decided she'd better pretend she loved six spoonfuls of sugar, and sipped her tea. As the taste registered on her tongue, she paused in surprise. It was perfect. He hadn't put in more than one teaspoonful, the bum. She cast him a secret look but he was focused on her grandparents as they stared at their glasses and squirmed. What did they expect to see, dirt?

Abigail lifted her glass almost to her lips, paused, then replaced it on the wicker tray. "Actually, we should be going." She checked her diamond-studded watch. "Didn't you tell the cabdriver to be back at three-thirty, Hubert? We ought to check in at the ship."

Her husband scanned his own watch, and once again Sally had the oddest feeling she was looking at little blue-blooded bookends. "The time does fly," Hubert murmured, pushing up to stand.

Noah set his glass on the tray and stood, too. "I think I hear the cab." He held out a hand and assisted Abigail to stand. "Now, don't be strangers."

"I—well..." Abigail smiled briefly then averted her gaze to settle her full attention on smoothing her skirt. As Sally labored to stand, Abigail's glance shot to her. "Oh, don't bother." She made a brisk, dismissing wave as though shooing a flea. "Your husband can see us to the door."

Sally sank back without argument. That was fine with her. Lately, getting out of chairs was hard enough when she really wanted to. "Have a nice cruise," she said, taking a sip of her tea. *Thank heavens!* The ordeal was almost over. Relaxing back, she closed her eyes.

A shriek and a thundering crash made them pop back open. The anguished howl that followed blasted her out of her chair.

CHAPTER TWO

NOAH felt an impact in his gut and looked down to see Abigail Vanderkellen sagging into him. Instinctively he scooped up the limp woman while he watched in shock as Hubert, who Abigail had apparently shoved in her initial panic, skidded across the entry tiles.

In a bizarre slow motion the elderly man toppled sideways into a metal sculpture that depicted what appeared to be a leafy, vining plant. With Mr. Vanderkellen's impact, the sculpture pitched over, causing a thunderous crash. Hubert quickly followed the sculpture to earth, his landing accompanied by a dull thud. After all motion ceased, Mr. Vanderkellen lay sprawled, faceup, arched awkwardly across the spiky metal.

His howl brought Noah out of his momentary astonishment and he hurriedly placed a swooning Mrs. Vanderkellen on the sofa. "See to your grandmother," he shouted at his fake wife as he rushed to Hubert.

Automatically he began a preliminary examination, wondering grimly when his workday would end and his long-anticipated vacation begin? This whole blasted day had been one time-consuming hassle after another. He'd thought he'd never get out of the hospital. When he pulled into Sam's sister's driveway, he'd been laboring under the delusion his headaches were over for the next two weeks. The cute pregnant lady who'd struggled down those steps hadn't given him any reason to change his mind. Not until she'd grabbed his hand, slipped a wedding ring onto his finger and whispered urgently that they were deliriously happy.

That's when he'd stepped into the Twilight Zone, and come face-to-face with a past he'd thought he'd left behind half a lifetime ago in Boston. He wasn't surprised that Abigail and Hubert hadn't immediately known him. After all, he'd left Massachusetts after graduating from high school and had only returned a few times to visit his family at Christmas. It was funny how life could deal you such crazy, surprising hands.

As he examined Hubert, he had the fleeting wish he was still dealing with last-minute hospital hassles. Since he'd come into Sam's sister's house a half hour ago, things had gone a little too nuts for his taste.

All he knew was, the pretty blonde, no doubt Sam's sister, was terribly uncomfortable around her grandparents. Why that was true, he couldn't imagine. He hadn't known the Vanderkellens well, but they had never seemed like demons. Just a little pompous. Still, her obvious dismay had been enough for him to go along with her wordless plea.

Those big, gray eyes had an uncanny effect on him. Or maybe it was her advanced pregnancy that was the deciding factor. Being an obstetrician, it would be natural for him to want to ease the stress of a woman in her condition—apparently even if he didn't have the faintest idea what in blazes he was doing.

He heard muted voices in the parlor and gathered Sam's sister was seeing to her grandmother, who was regaining consciousness. Thank goodness for that, at least. "We'll get you to a hospital, Mr. Vanderkellen, and—"

"No," the older man wheezed. "No hospital." He clutched Noah's arm. "I don't like hospitals—I don't need one."

"Don't move him!" came a worried female voice from the parlor. "We need to call an ambulance!"

Sam's sister appeared at the foyer entrance.

"How's your grandmother?"

"Feeling faint, but she's getting color back in her face." Her worried expression deepened. "What are you doing to Grandfather?" She hurried across the foyer and clutched Noah's shoulder as though attempting to make him back off. "You're *not* to move him until the ambulance arrives."

"This will go much faster if you don't grab at me." He leaned out of her grip.

"He needs a…" She paused. The next thing he knew she was whispering sharply in his ear. "He needs a *doctor!*"

"I know that." Noah turned to frown at her. He'd been at the hospital since 5:00 a.m. He was tired and he didn't feel like being grabbed, even if the grabber was attractive. "See if your grandmother would like a drink of water or a cool cloth for her head."

She looked upset and a warning blazed in her pretty eyes. "But—sweetie—*you* can't—"

"It's my bad back," Hubert broke in, moaning. "I've thrown it out, again. It's nothing—serious."

With the patient's admission of a chronic back problem, there was every indication medication and bed rest was all Hubert needed, but Noah tried again. "It would be better if you were examined at a hospital."

"*No!*" Hubert said gruffly, trying to prop himself up. "I won't have it. I detest those places." He winced, but refused to lie back.

"Okay, okay," Noah said. "Hold still. Let me help you." With great care, he lifted the man in his arms and carried him into the parlor. Mrs. Vanderkellen was now sitting, nervous fingers patted her hair. Clearly she wasn't a woman who lost her composure without suffering greatly for it.

"Sweetheart?" Noah tried not to grit his teeth with the lie.

His sham wife caught up. "Yes—dear?"

"Could you help your grandmother to that easy chair. It would be best if Hubert could lie flat."

"Oh…" His deliriously happy partner in crime didn't look deliriously happy as she scanned her pale grandmother. "Sure." She moved to the older woman's side. "Grandmother? May I help you to the chair?" She indicated the one she'd been sitting in. "Do you think you can make it?"

Mrs. Vanderkellen didn't look particularly delirious, either. "Of course, I'm fine." She eyed the floor as she was helped to the chair, as though expecting to see some beast leap out at her. Once she was seated, she lifted her feet to the ottoman and peered at Hubert. "Is it his back?"

Noah nodded. "I'm afraid so." He laid his moaning burden on the vacated couch. "You said this has happened before?"

"Yes." Hubert nodded, then closed his eyes in pain. "A muscle goes into spasms."

"When this happens," Noah asked, "what does your personal physician prescribe?"

"To stay active and walk it off," came a tart rejoinder from his wife.

Hubert made a face. "Complete bed rest and a muscle relaxant," he whispered through a moan, making it evident the effort to talk was agonizing. "I don't recall the name of the medication."

"He's faking!"

"Please, Mrs. Vanderkellen," Noah said, using his most compassionate bedside manner. "I need to talk to your husband."

She crossed her arms and flicked her gaze away, so he turned back to his patient. "Are you allergic to anything, sir?"

"No," Hubert whispered.

"Try to relax." Noah patted the man lightly on his shoulder. "I'll call in a prescription and have it sent over."

"Oh, Grandfather, I'm so sorry! I shouldn't have left that metal sculpture in the hallway."

Little Mrs. Expectant ducked in front of Noah, taking her grandfather's hand. He flinched and let out a long, elaborate groan.

"I don't recommend yanking on him," Noah said. "He's in severe distress." Turning away, he headed for the foyer where he'd seen a telephone table.

"I wasn't *yank*—where are you going? What are you doing?" she demanded.

The sound of sneakers squeaking on the wooden parlor floor told him she was catching up. He glanced her way, focusing on those big, worried eyes. "Your grandfather needs medication." Striding across the foyer, he reached the telephone table and lifted the receiver of the old, black telephone. "What's the nearest pharmacy?"

"Bert's Drugstore. Why?"

Deciding her question would be answered if she hung around listening, he dialed. "Information, give me the number for Bert's Drugstore."

"What are you doing?" she asked in a suspicious whisper.

"What does it sound like? I'm having a prescription— thank you, operator." He hung up with a finger on the disconnect button then dialed again.

"Are you crazy?" she demanded under her breath. "You can't—"

"Hush," he ordered, shifting away. "This is Dr. Noah Barrett, I need a prescription sent out to—" He paused, then remembered the scrap of paper Sam had written his sister's address on, and pulled it from his trouser pocket. "—to 95099 Bobolink Lane. It's at the end of the road. The prescription is for Hubert Vanderkellen."

As he told the pharmacist the medication and dosage, he felt several adamant yanks on his shirt. Exasperated, he peered over his shoulder. "What is it?"

"How dare you presume to make a diagnosis!" Mrs. Gray-Eyes charged, her whisper rough and low-pitched. "Phoning in a prescription and pretending to be a doctor is a criminal offense!"

The call completed, he hung up and scowled at her. Those huge eyes were round, horrified orbs the size of hula hoops. Her outraged expression stirred something in him and his annoyance receded a notch. "You told me I was a doctor," he said, with a wry twist of his lips. "If you keep changing the rules, I might get confused."

She gasped, her utter dismay curiously charming. He heard Mrs. Vanderkellen snap something to her husband, but couldn't make it out. "By the way..." He canted his head toward the parlor. "What got into your grandmother?"

"Don't change the subject! You can't go around phoning in prescriptions, pretending to be a doctor! You can go to jail for that kind of thing, buster!" She poked his chest. "That fifty bucks I'm paying you won't cover your bail."

"Fifty?" he asked, surprised and amused she'd planned to pay some stranger to play her husband.

"Don't even think about asking for more money!" She poked again. "And that kiss back there. That was way over the line!"

He grinned. "Want me to take it back?"

"Take it..." Her annoyed expression turned to confusion. "How?"

He lowered his head so his mouth was a couple of inches above hers. "Like this."

When he moved closer, his intent to kiss her made clear, she jerked away, her mouth forming an O at his audacity. "Look, you can be as supercilious as you want on your own time, but right now you're on my payroll."

He grinned. "Supercilious, huh? That's the first time I've ever been called that."

"It was the *nicest* word I could come up with on such short notice!"

He couldn't resist a low chuckle at her mettle. "Okay,

if you won't let me take the kiss back, let's call it even. You don't owe me any money.''

She looked startled, but misgiving continued to crinkle her forehead. ''Don't be silly. I pay my way. Now move. I'm calling an ambulance!''

''Your grandfather wants no part of hospitals and considering what he told me, I think he's right.''

''Oh, *you* think he's right, do you?'' Her sarcasm was so thick Noah would have been hard-pressed to cut it with a saw. ''I'm *so* relieved!''

A knock sounded at the door and the pregnant little chest-poker froze. ''Who could that be?''

How would he know? ''It's probably for me,'' Noah taunted.

She made a face at his gibe before turning toward the door. He had a feeling he knew who was at the door and halted her with a hand on her wrist while he fished his wallet out of his hip pocket. ''Give him this.''

She frowned in confusion, as he pulled out two twenties and a ten and stuffed them into her hand.

''What's this for?''

''Just hang on to it.''

She started to say something but another knock snapped her head around and she hurried to the door. ''Yes?''

Noah couldn't hear what was being said, but he could tell the visitor was a man.

''Oh!'' His hostess said in a half whisper. ''Oh, my...'' She stepped out on the porch and closed the door for a count of three, then was back. Her face had gone a rosy-peach color.

''Was it for me?'' he kidded with a lift of an eyebrow.

His question seemed to bring her out of some kind of daze and she flicked her attention to him. "No—it was—an orderly…"

"Did you give him the fifty?"

"He took it," she whispered, still looking befuddled. "He—he said I owed it…" After a second, her features closed in a glower. She walked to Noah and got as close as her pregnancy would allow. "Just who are you and what are you doing here?"

He frowned back, mocking her. "I tried to tell you when I got here."

The color drained from her face. "Why don't you tell me now?"

He checked his watch. Time was rapidly slipping away. "I'm a friend of Sam's, and if I'm going to catch my flight, I need to get out of here."

"Are you a—a real doctor, by chance?" she asked, her voice weak.

"Not by chance, by eight years of medical school."

That horrified look returned. She had gigantic eyes, a glimmery silver color he couldn't recall seeing before. Her white-blond hair was pulled back to her nape in a loose ponytail. Flyaway wisps framed her face in a feathery halo. Her right earlobe sported three studs, all silver, a heart, a ladybug and a hummingbird. Her left, just the heart. A bright pink T-shirt peeked out from beneath a paisley maternity dress. He could see her shapely legs from just above her knees down to purple crush socks and yellow, high-top canvas shoes.

She was nothing like he'd pictured Sam Johnson's little sister might be. Sam was a dark, quiet, button-down guy in wire-rimmed glasses. His doctorly regard gave nothing away. Noah seriously doubted Little Mrs. Bountiful, here, had kept an emotion to herself in her whole life.

She had an electricity about her that was distinct and magnetic. He could feel it arcing through the air, blunting his brain. That had to be it, since he couldn't imagine how his current circumstances would seem even vaguely palatable but for those big, animated eyes.

"So—so you're really a doctor?" The question was subdued and filled with astonishment, as though she'd just asked, *So you're really the Tooth Fairy?*

"I've got my doctor decoder ring and everything," he teased, taking pity on her, and unsure why. Possibly those big eyes, now a little teary.

"I thought you were—"

"I know. Forget it," he said. "Sam asked me to come by on my way to the airport to pick up his prescription goggles. The flight to Bonaire leaves in an hour, so I need to get to the airport." He stuck out a hand, deciding he had just enough time for a quick introduction. "I'm Noah Barrett. Sam and I are going scuba diving. Does that ring any bells?"

She swallowed and slipped her hand into his. He was startled to feel calluses on her palm, and her handshake was strong. What did this little female do all day, dig ditches? "Sam said something about scuba diving," she murmured. "I knew he was leaving on vacation today."

Noah cocked his head toward the parlor. "Did your grandmother tell you what caused her scare?"

It wasn't until the blonde removed her hand that Noah realized he hadn't let go. "She saw a gecko run by and apparently assumed it was some kind of plague-carrying,

Texas vermin.'' His fake wife shrugged, looking unhappy. "I guess it got in when I was outside with you. I think I convinced her the poor lizard wouldn't hurt her, and was more frightened than she was." She made a disgusted face. "Grandmother thinks Texas is a thousand miles away from civilization and expects to see man-eating rodents."

"I gathered they didn't come here for the sheer joy of it."

"*Why* they came is beyond me," she said. "The sooner we get them out of here, the better."

"They can't leave."

His statement drew her sharp gaze. "What—what do you mean they *can't* leave?"

"Your grandfather's in pain."

"What about a hospital? Pain is their thing!"

He watched her solemnly, wondering at her anxious hostility. "Hubert doesn't need hospitalization. Just bed rest. I don't think anyone could get him inside a hospital unless he was unconscious."

She glanced quickly toward the parlor, her expression a mix of belligerence and panic. "Well, he can't stay here."

"Why not? He's your grandfather."

"Because I don't want him here!"

Noah shook his head, baffled. "They're family."

"So? They never acted like family—not while..." She closed her mouth. "*Why* I don't want them here is not your concern."

She was absolutely right. Noah was vaguely curious about this new wrinkle, since as a boy he'd crossed the Vanderkellens' path at this-or-that Boston social function. But he didn't have time to indulge his curiosity. Bowing his head slightly, he ended the argument. "Have it your way. I'll get Sam's goggles and go."

He indicated the direction of the kitchen. "Sam thought they might be on the screened porch. I assume it's back there?"

The blonde's furrowed brow didn't ease. "I haven't seen them, but yes, the porch is off the kitchen." She waved him away, making it clear she had more urgent problems to contend with. "Check if you want."

He took a step, then stopped. "By the way," he whispered. "What's your name?"

She blinked as though being dragged back from some dark place. "What?"

"Your name?"

"Oh—Sally—Sally Johnson."

He was surprised she was single, but he supposed he shouldn't be. He'd seen a lot of single mothers in his practice. It was only that, knowing Sam and how smart and logical he was, Noah wouldn't have thought his sister would be quite so uncircumspect. "Well, good luck, Sally."

She pressed her fingertips to her temples and closed her eyes, exhaling. When Noah faced the fact she either hadn't heard him or didn't intend to respond, he went in search of the goggles.

Five minutes of searching around, under and behind a platform glider, stacked scraps of metal, a bike, gardening tools, flower pots and a potting bench, finally brought success. Noah returned to the foyer, the goggles jutting from his hip pocket. Nobody was in the entry, but he heard voices in the parlor. When he looked in to say goodbye he was met by those blasted shimmery eyes, another silent plea hitting him full force.

"Everything okay?" he found himself asking.

She motioned him inside. "Uh—honey—could you take grandfather up to my—er—our room? He and grandmother will be staying."

Noah felt a hitch in his chest at her use of the endearment. For a moment, he'd forgotten their charade. He gave his watch a quick, worried look. "Well—sure."

"This is ridiculous," Mrs. Vanderkellen said. "You never wanted to go on the walking tour of the pyramids! I should have known you'd—"

Hubert's loud moan cut off his wife's tirade. He clutched at his lower back. *"Oh, the pain!"*

"He took a pretty bad fall," Noah interjected.

Mrs. Vanderkellen slid Noah a dubious look, as though he were part of some demonic conspiracy, but didn't voice her suspicions. "It will take an outrageous tip to get that cabbie to move the bags in off the drive," she muttered. "Noah, handle that."

After taking care of the driver, Noah trudged up the stairs with his spindly burden, depositing Hubert in Sally's sunny room on a patchwork quilt decorating a pine four-poster. "After he gets some medication, I'll help you get him into bed."

Mrs. Vanderkellen rummaged in her purse and didn't immediately answer. When she turned around she held a canister of some sort. Instead of responding to his offer, she began to fog the air with what smelled like disinfectant.

Ducking under the reeking jet, he left the room and

nearly crashed into Sally, lurking in the hall, wringing her hands.

"So, you're letting them stay after all," he said. "That's nice."

"Nice?" she echoed, clearly miserable. "They told me their house in Boston is being completely redecorated. They think all but a handful of hotels are filthy places teeming with the germs of a thousand strangers. And not surprisingly, not one of those *adequate* hotels is in this country. Oh, and they wouldn't consider imposing on friends. Can you believe that? They don't want to impose on *friends!* But, me, they can impose on."

"They're family—"

"Look, Dr. Garrett," she cut in. "I'm sure you have a warm and fuzzy relationship with your grandparents, and I'm sure they're as sweet as teddy bears. But not everybody is that lucky."

He didn't have time to get into a discussion about his family dynamics, though he had a feeling she'd be surprised about a few details if he did. So he merely corrected, "It's Barrett."

"What?"

He shook his head. "Never mind. It was interesting to meet you, Sally." He loped down the stairs, racing the clock.

"Oh—wait! *Please!*"

His plan to make a swift exit was thwarted by his hostess's entreaty. When he turned, she was lumbering down the stairs, a protective hand on her stomach. Her descent was precariously rapid and he automatically headed in her direction.

"Don't—you'll fall." He jogged up several steps and took her arm. "What's so important?"

"You—can't go!" she said, short of breath. Pulling him into the parlor, she added, "What do I tell them?"

Noah was confused. "About what?"

"About us—being deliriously happy!"

He stared at her, not believing this. Their playacting had been amusing for a few minutes, but now it was just strange. "Look—Sally was it?" He separated her desperate, clutching fingers from his shirt front and took off the wedding ring she'd given him. "I don't care what you tell them." Plunking it into her hand, he went on. "I've been looking forward to a vacation for three years. *Three years,*" he repeated. "My flight leaves in forty-five minutes. Tell your grandparents whatever you want. Tell them I had to go to a medical convention. Or aliens beamed me up to the mother ship. I don't care." He closed her fingers over the wedding band, and squeezed as a parting gesture. "Have a good life."

She made a pained face. "I'll pay you!"

"I don't want your money."

"What do you want? I'll do anything!" she cried. "Don't you see? They think I'm inferior. They think my mother married beneath her, that my dad was some kind of inferior subspecies just because he was a firefighter from Texas and not old money from Boston. If they find out I'm having a baby and I'm not married—well, they'll be convinced I'm the riffraff they predicted."

"Riffraff?" Noah was astonished by such a crazy statement. "I doubt that. I'd have to agree raising a child without a stable, two-parent family is hardly ideal, but

I'm sure you're making more out of their reaction than—"

"I'm not! You don't know me or my grandparents, so you can keep your opinions to yourself! Doctors!" she scoffed. "Insufferable know-it-alls, every last one of you." She eyed him angrily. "Why I'm having this baby is my business, not my grandparents' or *yours*."

"If you'll recall, you dragged me into it."

"That was my mistake," she said. "But I'm not making a mistake about my grandparents' attitude. They're the world's most self-righteous, narrow-minded, class-conscious, stuffy snobs!" She pressed her fists against her temples. "I won't let them blame any decisions I've made on inferior *Johnson* genes. I couldn't stand seeing their revolted expressions if they knew the father of my baby came from a freezer in a sperm bank, and a glorified turkey baster played cupid!"

Noah was startled to hear there was no man in the picture. She was pretty enough to have her pick of daddies for her child. He wondered why she'd opted to get pregnant at all, let alone by artificial insemination. Maybe she didn't like men. Whatever the reason, it wasn't his concern. "Look, I can see you're upset, and I feel for you, but this isn't a good time."

She stared at him for a heartbeat, her pinched expression making it clear she didn't buy his "I feel for you" remark. Maybe she was more correct in her assessment than he cared to admit. Single motherhood was a tough row to hoe. To choose it voluntarily was highly unorthodox and questionable. If Miss Johnson was like too many of his single-parent patients, she hadn't given adequate thought to what she was getting herself—and an innocent child—into.

"Right." Heaving an exhale, she threw up her hands in defeat. "It's not your problem and you've got a plane to catch." She indicated her grandparents' bags. "But could you—er—take those up, first? There's no way my grandmother could do it—or even consider it—and I don't think I could get that trunk upstairs without going into premature labor."

He shot the pile of luggage an unfriendly glare, but hesitated for only a second. Somehow he knew arguing with this little dynamo would merely waste time. "Okay. All right," He headed for the suitcases. "Then I'm gone."

The phone rang, but Noah paid little heed. His focus was on the eight matching leather suitcases and one steamer trunk the size of a compact car. Exactly how long had the Vanderkellens planned to be away on their cruise. Four years?

"It's for you," Sally held out the receiver. "Somebody named Jane. Says it's important."

He stopped in the middle of hefting the trunk. "Jane?" His girlfriend was at the airport with Sam and his fiancée, Dorothy. Maybe their flight had been delayed. For once that would be good news.

He lowered the trunk to the foyer tiles and took the device from Sally's outstretched hand.

"I'll get your fifty," Sally whispered.

He shook his head, covering the mouthpiece. "It won't do you any good. I won't take it." Noah made a point of turning away to indicate the subject was closed. "Hi, honey. What's up?"

"Sugar!" came a familiar, breathy voice. "We're waiting. What's keeping you?"

"I'm just—"

"Noah, you *have* to get here. I've got a wonderful surprise for you!"

He didn't doubt that, and grinned. When he started to reassure her, she rushed on. "Oh, I can't stand it. I have to tell!"

His grin faded. This was wasting time, but he knew better than to try to stop Jane in the middle of a gush.

"Lovey," she said, sounding coy. "I've made a slight change in the itinerary." Her pause was just drawn-out enough for Noah to experience a prick of apprehension. "Dorothy told me about Bonaire, and I'm sure you didn't realize there's absolutely no night life there. Nothing but scuba diving."

"That's what we're doing," he reminded her, experiencing a twinge of irritation. "Remember, you said you wanted to learn."

"Well, sure, but I thought we'd do that one afternoon, maybe two. I didn't think you meant to scuba dive day in and day out for the whole vacation!" Her voice had taken on a slight whine. "Noah, with my delicate skin, I can't spend a lot of time in the sun. That's why I changed our reservations to the most scrumptious hotel on Aruba. You'll adore it. Aruba isn't that far away from Bonaire. You can maybe meet Sam and Dorothy a couple of mornings to dive while I sleep in. It'll be absolute heaven!"

Noah heard his vacation plans getting flushed, but couldn't believe it. "You're kidding, right?" he said with a light laugh, presuming this was her idea of a joke.

He hadn't been diving since college and was excited about starting again. For a long time he'd been searching for an antidote for the stress and long hours of his work. Something to balance out a career he loved, but found too all-consuming. He needed peace, a quiet place to go and rest, both physically and emotionally. The cool, silent primeval depths of the ocean seemed perfect.

His first effort in finding emotional peace had been his relationship with Jane. She was beautiful, always ready for fun. But after two years, he was starting to realize something was missing.

"Kidding?" she asked. "Why would I kid, Noah? We can do our thing and they can do theirs. Doesn't it sound like heaven?"

He experienced a tightening in his gut as the detestable truth hit. "No, Jane," he muttered. "It doesn't."

"What?"

Noah could almost laugh at the disbelief in her tone. She had no idea he might be angry, that he would consider what she'd done to be self-centered, high-handed manipulation. Just two months before, to Jane's dismay, he'd turned down a plum job at Boston's Women's Hospital. According to her, in her invariable whine, "the Barrett name means something in Boston! You could *do* anything you want, be *important* there!" To appease her, he'd been forced to get Sam to cover for him while he took her on a long, romantic weekend in Las Vegas.

Yeah, he knew all about the Barrett name and the obligatory pomp and circumstance that came with it in Boston society. That was a major reason he'd left to attend the University of Texas, then Baylor's College of Medicine. By the time he graduated he'd lost his Boston accent, loved the casual comfort of cowboy boots, so he'd stayed on to open his ob-gyn practice in Houston. The Barrett name didn't mean a hill of beans in Houston. Besides, he liked his patients, especially the cases he saw one day a week when he volunteered at a charity clinic.

He remembered how Jane had complained, ''But you can have your precious charity cases in Boston, too!'' Noah didn't bother to explain his feelings—that his patients were not merely names on files, but flesh and blood, and they depended on him.

At this moment he was not only furious and frustrated, but suddenly weary of the high-maintenance relationship with Jane. He needed a little space, some time to calm down. With a gritted curse, he caught sight of Sally Johnson, trudging up the stairs, lugging one of the bags. He frowned as a bizarre thought struck.

''Sweetie?'' Jane's query drew him back. ''Where did you go?''

''Put Sam on,'' he muttered, the vague beginnings of an idea forming in his mind.

''What?''

''Put Sam on, Jane,'' he repeated, working to hold his temper.

He heard her call Sam. As he waited he ground his teeth.

''Hey, buddy, can't find the goggles?''

''I found them.''

''Good. See you soon.''

''I don't think so.'' Noah was not ordinarily an impulsive man. But right now he was angry, so he wasn't quite himself. ''Your sister asked me to do her a favor,'' he said, deciding to go with the impulse and let the chips fall where they may. "Tell Jane to enjoy herself. I'll join her as soon as I can." Literal translation, *When I cool off.*

Sam laughed. "Very funny."

"I'm serious. I'll mail your goggles."

There was a pause. "Jane's going to be royally ticked."

"That'll make two of us."

"She told you?"

"Yeah."

Sam cleared his throat. "I'm sorry, man. I didn't know what she'd done until we got here." In the silence that followed, Noah sensed Sam was working to keep from speaking disparagingly about his best friend's girl. "So—what's this favor you're doing for my sister?"

"No big deal." Angry and restless, he shoved a hand through his hair. "I'm just going to be her husband."

CHAPTER THREE

SALLY lugged the heavy bag up the steps, trying to ignore the telephone conversation going on in the foyer. It wasn't hard. The doctor had lowered his voice, so she couldn't hear what was being said no matter how hard she strained—not that she *was* straining.

She fought off a wish that the plane had mechanical problems and her phony husband wouldn't be able to leave right away. Maybe with a little reprieve she'd have time to come up with some plausible reason for him to be going out of town. A medical conference did seem like a workable idea.

"What a mess," she muttered as she lugged the bag one step at a time. It thudded into the riser of each oncoming step as she labored, dragging and bouncing it to each, new level. Out of nowhere, a hand swept in to relieve her of the burden. Luckily she had a firm grip on the worn banister or she'd have tumbled backward in surprise.

"Hi," Noah said, his expression less than delighted.

"I've got this one," she said. "If you could just get the trunk before you go."

"I'm not going." His nostrils flared as he ground out the statement. "Not today."

She stared, confused. "Did—did something go wrong with the airplane?"

He shook his head. "I just decided…" He shrugged.

"Sam did me a favor a couple of months ago. I figured I could help out his sister for a day or two. Pay him back." He shifted the bag to his other side and held out a hand. "Better give me that ring."

She felt cotton-headed. "Ring?"

One corner of his mouth quirked upward, but there was no humor in his eyes. "With this ring, I thee wed?"

"Oh…" She found herself wholly focused on that cynical half smile as she listened to him repeat a line of the wedding vows. An unruly warmth sang through her body, and she wondered at her bizarre reaction. She'd never been through a wedding, though she'd been engaged. To a doctor. For a short time. But as pregnant as she was, standing beside this stranger, his lips twisted sardonically as he gruffly spoke a handful of sacred words, her heart did an odd series of flip-flops.

She shook herself. *Sally Johnson get a grip. The man is being sarcastic. Besides, you look like a double-decker bus with a head!* Belatedly, and fearful the burning in her cheeks meant she was blushing, she fished her daddy's wedding ring from her pocket and handed it to him. "I—I don't know how to thank you, Dr. Garrett."

He lay the bag down, slid the ring onto his left hand, then scowled her way. "First, the name's Barrett, not Garrett, and second, call me Noah."

"Shouldn't I—probably call you sweetheart or honey—like we did in the parlor?"

He picked up the luggage. "Call me whatever your idea of 'deliriously happy' is. Only quit calling me Dr. Garrett."

"What are you going to call me?"

He'd taken a step up, but with her question he turned.

That magnetic, twisted grin reappeared. "What about sugarplum? That has a deliriously happy ring to it."

She wrinkled her nose. "Too gooey."

He chuckled, the sound rich and deep. He was laughing at her, but for some reason it didn't matter to her raging hormones. Another rush of heat washed over her. "You look like a sugarplum to me," he said.

She frowned at his taunting. "Round and purple?"

He grinned, this time it wasn't crooked or skewed, but with his whole mouth, if not his eyes. Even as half-hearted as the pleasant expression was, the effect made her catch her breath. "Not purple," he said, then turned away. "More like fuchsia."

She didn't know why that last remark struck her as funny. Clearly he was taunting her. Still, she found herself fighting a smile. "I'd rather you call me honey or sweetheart."

"Check—sugarplum."

She experienced a prick of annoyance at his reckless disobedience and frowned at him as he climbed the steps. For some crazy reason, she couldn't drag her gaze away. She wondered why. It certainly wasn't the way his trousers fit across his backside, or the sly impression against khaki of taut muscle, shifting and bunching in his thighs and calves, as he moved.

Irritated with herself, she made a face. 'Don't lust after the doctor, Sally," she mumbled. "Remember the last doctor you…" She clamped her jaws and headed down the steps to fetch another bag. She needed to concentrate on how she and Dr. Garrett—er—*Barrett* were going to carry off this farce.

Her little deception had seemed so easy, so foolproof,

when it had just been for an hour. Who would have guessed things could get this fouled up?

As she stepped to the foyer tiles, a knock sounded at the door. She answered it to find the pharmacy delivery boy. She'd just closed the door when Noah reappeared, taking the stairs two at a time. To her great dismay, he looked every bit as sexy coming down as he did going up.

The baby kicked, and she winced. "Right. The doctor's sexiness is none of our business."

"Did you say something to me?"

She shook her head, fearing she wasn't quite able to vanquish her sheepish expression. "I was talking to little Vivica." She patted her stomach.

His thundercloud expression cleared slightly. "A girl?"

She nodded, taking the prescription from the bag and scratching at the name Barrett until it was mutilated and unreadable. "That's probably something you should know."

"What the hell are you doing?" he asked.

She peeled the little sticker off that said something about not driving while taking the medicine and restuck it over the rubbed and smudged area where the word Barrett had been. "What does it look like I'm doing, Dr. *Step?*"

With her emphasis on their fake married name, he got it. "Oh, right. Good thinking."

"Thanks." She replaced the prescription in the bag. "And, by the way, Vivica was my mother's name."

"The Vanderkellens's daughter?"

"Right. And the baby's middle name's Charlotte. Daddy's mother's name. Grandmother and grandfather wouldn't know that, but you should."

"And when's little Vivica Charlotte Step due?"

"Four weeks. April 1." She raised a hand when he started to speak. "I know. I know. It's April Fool's Day, but Vivica has *promised* to be a little early or a little late." She held out the pharmacy bag. "Here you go."

He scooped up a couple of suitcases. "You and Vivica take it to him. I'll finish with these." He started up, then glanced back. "My bag is in my truck. Where do you want me to stow it?"

Sally was momentarily stymied. She hadn't thought about the consequences of her fake husband staying on—*an actual physical presence needing actual physical space.* Drat! Why had Abigail Vanderkellen shoved Hubert into that sculpture? It had to be bad karma. Obviously, since she'd decided to lie, she was going to pay *big!* "Uh—I guess—the room upstairs at the end of the hall."

He nodded. "Check."

Sally was suddenly smacked in the face with a daunting reality. Miserable and shaky, she lowered herself to sit on a step. Other than the nursery, which at the moment had no bed in it at all, the room at the end of the hall was the *only* other bedroom in the house. Unfortunately for them both, Noah Barrett would be forced to share it with an extremely pregnant roommate.

Sally dropped her head in her hands, praying that her hired husband would take the news well. Or failing that, at least take it quietly.

The afternoon was long; tension filled the air. Hubert spent most of his time moaning and insisting he couldn't move while Abigail spent her time insisting he get up and ''walk it off.''

Sally cleared out some closet space, explaining the lack of masculine clothing in a vague statement that they were in the middle of ''rearranging things for the baby.'' Not that Abigail cared or even listened. She spent most of her time glaring at Hubert and spraying disinfectant.

Noah had been quiet and grim when out of sight of the Vanderkellens. He'd made one trip into town to pick up food for Abigail's ''delicate palate.'' Which, translated, meant she assumed anything already opened in Sally's refrigerator was contaminated.

Sally took a dinner tray of newly purchased cottage cheese, peach slices and freshly ground designer coffee to her grandmother. As she trekked back downstairs, she wondered if Abigail's need to eat beside Hubert's bedside was because she was so devoted, or because she hadn't disinfected the kitchen.

She reentered the kitchen surprised to see Noah standing at the gas range, stirring the ingredients in her frying pan. At the sound of her entry, he glanced toward the door, his expression closed and unreadable.

She still reeled at his decision to forgo the first few days of his precious vacation to help her. Whatever the favor Sam had done for Noah must have been a whopper. It was clear he was far from happy he'd made this choice. Maybe she would ask what tipped the scales in her favor. Later. Right now she opted for a more immediate question. ''What are you doing to the fried potatoes and onions?''

''They were starting to stick.''

She was amazed he'd noticed. Black smoke could have been billowing out, filling the room with choking smog and Sam wouldn't have registered any problem. "Thanks." She took the cooking fork from his hand. "I think the meat loaf is ready. We could eat."

"What about a salad?"

She peered at him. She wasn't a salad person, but she'd tried hard to include them in her diet. On occasion. "Uh, I don't know what I have…but if you want one…" She waved the cooking fork toward the refrigerator, giving permission to look.

He indicated her belly, covered by a color-happy, ruffled apron. "I think some raw greens would be good for Vivica."

Sally wasn't accustomed to having anybody tell her what to do, but she held her temper. After all, Noah was doing her a favor. "Well—if you can find anything saladlike, feel free."

He rummaged through the refrigerator. "So, how's your grandfather?"

"Asleep. I think in self-defense. Unconscious he can't hear grandmother accusing him of malingering."

Noah's deep, cynical chuckle filled the air. "I gathered from what I heard, the first week of their cruise included an extensive walking tour of the pyramids of Cozumel. I got the strong impression Hubert was *not* particularly hot for it."

"The second week is supposed to take them to St. Martin, St. Thomas and Martinique where, according to Abigail, Hubert planned to play golf, golf and more golf, which she abhors with a passion."

Noah straightened and it appeared from Sally's vantage point at the stove, that he'd found a few items that might be considered saladish. "Sounds to me like you can count on Hubert recovering in a week."

She exhaled wearily and shook her head. "I may kill myself before then."

She heard a noise and turned to see Noah depositing a small, wilting stalk of celery on the green-tiled countertop along with a handful of pebbles that might once have been radishes. He'd also found a bruised, overripe tomato and half a head of cauliflower that didn't look too bad.

"Do you have any canned vegetables?" he asked.

She couldn't stifle a small smile. "Why? You're a doctor. Can't you save those?"

He grinned back, and Sally's breath caught. Even without employing his eyes in the pleasant expression, he had the most outrageously magnetic show of teeth she'd ever seen. She wondered what his bedside manner might be like, then clamped down on such daydreams. *No lewd thoughts, Sally girl,* she told herself. *You're about to become a mama. Your thoughts should be maternal, not carnal!*

"These are okay, but I thought I'd add some green beans or carrots or something."

She aimed her cooking fork at a narrow pine door next to the exit to the back porch. "Take a look."

He did, and after a few seconds of scrounging, came out with a couple of cans. "Corn and peas," he said.

She made a face. "Sounds like a disgusting combination. Are you sure Vivica needs to be put through that? I'm taking prenatal vitamins like a good little soldier."

"Humor me."

She wrinkled her nose and turned away. "The potatoes are done."

"This won't take long."

Sally set two places at the Formica and metal table, then transferred the meat loaf and potatoes to serving dishes. Noah placed his rendition of a salad on the table at the same time she lay down the rest of the meal.

She examined the bowl of veggies with misgivings. "I never thought to ask you if you could cook."

"No need. I'm extraordinary." He swept a hand across the salad. "This is a perfect example of my culinary mastery."

"That's what I'm afraid of." She noticed he'd put some kind of dressing on it and was curious what it was, but decided not to ask. "What do you want to drink? I'm having ice water."

"I'm good with that."

She fixed two glasses and placed them on the table. As she started to seat herself, she was startled by his helping hand on the back of her chair. "That's not necessary," she said, a little abashed. She'd made derogatory remarks about his salad idea and maligned his abilities as a cook, and here he was being a gentleman.

"You're my dearly beloved, aren't you?" he kidded, taking his own seat.

She eyed him as she spooned up a helping of fried potatoes and onions. "Are you some kind of method actor?"

He served them both big helpings of salad. Sally had the feeling he was going to make her eat it. "Actually," he said, "I tend to try to give aid and comfort to pregnant women. It's one of the hazards of being an obstetrician.''

She was surprised. ''Oh—I...'' She shrugged as he took the potatoes and served himself. ''With grandfather's fall and all, I figured you were an orthopedist or something.''

''You thought I was an orderly.''

She felt her cheeks go hot. ''That joke has stopped being funny.''

His lips quirked and he nodded. ''Check. No longer funny.''

After they began to eat, silence ruled for a painfully long period. The only sounds were the occasional clink of stainless-steel flatware against Sally's mother's terracotta pottery.

''So, Sally...'' Clearing his throat, Noah amended, ''I mean, *sugarplum*...'' His teasing glance caught and held hers. ''Since we're alone for the moment, do you mind satisfying my curiosity about something?''

She experienced a twinge of uneasiness and swallowed her bite of meat loaf. ''If you're groping for a compliment about the salad. It's just fine. What's the dressing?''

His mouth did that crooked-grinning-thing again, and she had to shift her attention to her plate to regroup.

''It's my own blend of olive oil, balsamic vinegar, salt and pepper and dried oregano, but—''

''*Balsamic* vinegar?'' She asked. ''Where did you find anything like that here?''

He indicated a pretty blue bottle in the window. ''Right there.''

She stared at it. ''Is that what that is?''

"What did you think it was?"

"I didn't care. I bought it because it was pretty. I liked the blue glass and the cheerful sprig of rosemary inside."

"Now you know it's pretty, cheerful balsamic vinegar, but when I said I'd like you to satisfy my curiosity, I was referring to the unorthodox pregnancy."

She shot him a suspicious look. "Why? It's a perfectly legitimate way to get pregnant! Do you have a problem with it?"

His smile remained crookedly handsome, but his brow crinkled, as though her sharp query surprised him. "Not in theory." He nodded. "But since you're single, I simply wondered what prompted such an extreme life choice?"

"What's so extreme?" She lifted her chin, defiant. "I want a baby. I don't want some casual acquaintance staking any claim on her, complicating my life. So I went to a sperm bank. Simple."

"Ah." His brow remained crinkled, as though dubious about her reasoning. "Simplicity."

She would not let herself be questioned or put down by this guy—this virtual stranger! How dare he challenge her choices! "Yes, *simplicity*. If it's any of your business, it's very simple. First, I love children. Second, I have no commitment-oriented man in my life, and third, I'm about to turn twenty-eight."

One brow rose in obvious skepticism. "I see."

She pulled her gaze away and stabbed a cauliflower bud. "You don't have to like it *or* understand it."

"I realize that," he said, drawing her glare. "Except, in my practice I see the results of single-parenthood daily. Too many young women take on a child to raise by themselves these days without the maturity or knowledge of what being a single mother requires. They want a doll to play with, or somebody to love them. They don't understand the money, time, energy and patience necessary to raise a child alone.'' He leaned slightly forward, resting the flats of his hands on the table. To Sally the move seemed aggressive. ''That's why, when I see an attractive young woman with years and years ahead of her to make a real family, and I discover she's made a conscious choice to have a child, alone, I can't help but ask myself if she knows what the hell she's doing.''

His patronizing speech sent her over the edge. Her composure blew sky high. ''Well, *sugar-lump,* ask away—as long as you keep your questions strictly to yourself. For the record, *Dr.* Barrett, I don't need a lecture and I *sure* don't need a father, and neither does my baby!'' Slamming her hands on the tabletop she pushed up, which in her condition was no easy feat. ''For the next few days I need a husband. It's just too bad for both of us, you're it.''

Untying her apron, she flung it over the back of her chair, angry with herself for being so offended and hurt by his narrow-minded attitude. He was as bad as her grandparents. It appeared she'd jumped from the frying pan right into the fire. ''Doctors! I swear, if one ever admits to being wrong, the world would end!''

''Calm down,'' he said, pushing up to stand. ''You're wound so tight you might as well be an alarm clock.''

''How tightly I'm wound is none of your business, either!''

''As an obstetrician, and because you're very pregnant, I'm making it my business. You don't have to like it.''

"Well, I don't like it, so don't even try!" she warned, muttering, *"Pompous know-it-all!"*

"Don't think I didn't hear that."

"Don't think I care!" She lurched away. "I'm going to take a hot bath." Kneading her aching back, she plodded out of the kitchen. "Leave the dishes. I'll do them later."

"Not hot," he called. "Tepid!"

Muttering lively and explicit suggestions about what he could do with his tyranny, she trudged up the stairs.

After a chilly bath, Sally sterilized her bathroom to the best of her ability and peeked in the sickroom to tell her grandmother it was free. Hubert lay flat on his back, snoring rhythmically.

"Should I bring up any food for Grandfather?" she asked, a last-minute thought.

"No," Abigail said, her mouth pinched so tightly it looked as if it had been surgically removed, leaving only a small scar. "He can just get up and feed himself."

Sally took a deep, calming breath. "But—well, if he needs anything, let me know."

Abigail harrumphed. "The old fraud. If it were a golf tournament he'd shake off that preposterous backache!" She waved Sally away. "Go to bed. He won't starve to death during the night."

Sally closed the door, and walked down the stairs. She was ready for bed, in her flannel nightgown and floor-length terry robe. This early March evening had blown in a cool front and the temperature had dropped significantly. As she descended, her fuzzy scuffs made slapping sounds on the stairs.

The last thing she wanted to do was wash a sinkful of greasy dishes, but leaving them until breakfast would only make the job more distasteful.

She flipped on the kitchen light and was startled to find the room in pristine order. Not a dirty dish in sight. So, the doctor had cleaned up, had he? She folded her arms over Vivica. "Hmm," she said, experiencing a twinge of guilt she was extremely unhappy to admit. She'd been quite a shrew when she'd stomped out of the kitchen. Even so, he'd stayed and washed the dishes, even put them away.

"No doubt part and parcel of his threat to make my pregnancy his business," she groused. She found some comfort in her annoyance, now that she'd decided his cleaning up was a piece of his dark plot to manipulate her. Doctors! They all had God complexes. They were right and everybody else was wrong. Her brother, Sam, might be a doctor, but he loved her the way she was, making him a pleasant, rare exception to the rule.

The embers of her animosity stirred and flickering, she headed back upstairs. Her hand was on the doorknob of her room before she remembered that, for the immediate future, the room was not hers. She pivoted on her scuffs and tramped to the end of the hall. That door was closed. She started to knock, but the rattle of the bathroom door signaled her grandmother's exit from the bathroom, so she changed her mind.

Sally grasped the knob and turned, offering her grandmother a brief nod and civil smile before she slipped inside. When she closed the door, she was met with the sight of her pompous, overbearing pretend-husband, lounging on the edge of the double bed, its iron head and footboard of a similar leafing and vining design to the sculpture that had caused all the havoc.

Sally had always thought the airy, outdoor theme of her ironwork was rather feminine. But right now, the taut brawn of a muscular male slouched there. To make matters worse, he wore nothing but a pair of randomly striped boxers that gave the impression of a loincloth. Why then, because a nearly naked Noah Barrett entered the mix, did her pretty, feminine bed suddenly become the spitting image of Tarzan's jungle lair?

Apparently hearing the door click shut, he glanced up, his grim, preoccupied expression changing to one of surprise.

He wasn't the only one to be shocked. "Oh—" She plastered herself against the door in an instinctive attempt to give him and all his bare skin some space. Which didn't substitute for privacy but it was the best she could do.

She made a point of looking at the ceiling fan, its white blades slowly turning to circulate the cool evening breeze. "I—I couldn't knock. Grandmother…uh…came out of the bathroom. I'm sorry."

"What can I do for you?" he asked quietly.

She shifted her gaze to the front window, trying to concentrate on the white lacy curtains waving toward the bed, as though they were saying, *"Look at him! Isn't he cute? Take a good, long look!"* She scowled at the window for its lewd suggestion. "Actually," she began, then cleared her throat to steady her scratchy voice. "I forgot to tell you something."

"What?"

He sounded a tad irritated. Could she blame him?

"That—uh—" She made a pained face, her concentration on the window faltering. "Could you—would you mind putting on some *clothes?*"

"I have on some clothes."

"That—I—um…" She shook her head, wishing she'd had the presence of mind to tell him the whole, unhappy truth after dinner, before she stalked out of the kitchen. "No, you don't have on some clothes."

He stood up. She knew that because the bedsprings squeaked. "How long is this going to take?"

She fought to keep from looking at him. "Why?"

"So I'll know how dressed to get."

She swallowed hard. "Just—just put on whatever you wear to bed."

"That would require taking *off* what I'm wearing." He paused, possibly to gape in amazement at the bright crimson color of her face. "I'm decent enough," he said. "Think of them as jogging shorts."

She heaved a sigh and propped her hands at the small of her aching back. She might as well bite the bullet and get this over. "Well, I…" She shook her head, searching for the best way to break the news. "It's just that…"

She heard him pad across the pine planks until the billowing curtains were blocked by a close-up view of his chest. It was an extremely nice chest as male chests go.

"It's just that what?" he asked.

Her glance did a slow, reluctant climb to meet his quizzical stare.

"We're, uh, going to have to sleep together?" It came out like a question—a high-pitched, unhappy question.

For a long, nerve-racking moment his stare didn't change. Sally heard the curtains behind him snap in the breeze. Even that small sound made her wince in anticipation of his enraged explosion. At long last, she detected movement as his brows dipped. He pursed his lips. "You're telling me this is the *only* other bedroom."

She nodded, chewing the inside of her cheek. "Except for the nursery. But there's no bed…" Allowing the sentence to fade away, she went back to nervously chewing. "And—and—and we're supposed to be deliriously happily—married." Fearing he might bolt and run, she hastily added, "Remember, you agreed to help me."

He seemed to contemplate her reminder for another endless moment. "It's coming back to me," he said at last, his lips twitching into that cynical, sexy smile. "Okay—sugarplum…" He backed up and held out his arms as though putting himself on display. "No matter how unpalatable the prospect may be, you might as well get used to looking at the shorts." Lowering his arms, he hooked a thumb under the waistband. "Or looking at me." His crooked grin taunted. "You choose."

CHAPTER FOUR

NOAH watched Sally's complexion turn a shocked pink, and berated himself for teasing her with the suggestion he might take off his shorts. She was already dealing with a set of unwelcome, fussy grandparents. Moreover, she was extremely pregnant and emotional. Why was he fooling around? He wasn't normally into ribbing pregnant women.

He lifted his hands in surrender. "Sorry. I was kidding."

Her reaction was little more than a blink. Deciding he'd better get his attitude adjusted, he swept a hand toward the bed, covered with forest-green chenille. A weird thought struck—it looked less like a place to sleep than a woodland clearing. All it needed was a babbling brook. "Which is my side?" He started to add sugarplum, but decided she'd had enough trauma for one day. When she didn't immediately respond, he glanced her way. "Or do you expect me to camp on the floor?"

He could tell by her unhappy expression she leaned in that direction. He wasn't surprised, but he didn't relish wrapping himself in a blanket on the pine planks. Even the quaint rag rug that took up much of the floor in front of the bed didn't look very inviting.

She heaved a sigh and shook her head. "No. You're doing me a favor. You deserve to sleep on the bed." She faced him, her features determined, cautioning. "I don't have to remind you the sleeping arrangement is purely platonic." She started to say more, made a couple of false starts, but didn't seem to be able to find words, or choked at having to say them. He had a feeling her difficult statement was something like, *"I'm not particularly alluring, anyway, so I don't expect you to jump me,"* but she evidently decided to drop it. He was glad. Sally Johnson was alluring, whether she knew it or not. However, since she was reluctantly allowing him into her bed, it would be unwise to say anything that might make her rethink her offer.

"Well?" she prodded, drawing him from his reverie.

"Hmm? Oh, right. Platonic. Absolutely."

She wagged a hand toward the side of the mattress nearest the door. "I'll sleep there, if you don't mind. It's closer to the bathroom."

He nodded. "No problem. Pregnancy does have its little inconveniences."

She shrugged. "Spoken like a man."

He eyed her dubiously. "I thought this pregnancy was your idea."

As she rounded the bed, she peered at him. "I was being sexist, not griping about my decision."

He found that remark curiously endearing. "Ah, insult humor." He faked a wince. "Ouch."

His attempt at levity crashed and burned. Her features remained somber as she pulled back the spread and gave him a look. "Would you help me fold this back?"

There was no mistaking the fact that sharing a bed with him didn't thrill her to her core. He adopted an equally somber expression. "At your service, ma'am."

She gave him a sharp, suspicious look. "This isn't funny."

He pursed his lips and nodded. "Not at all. No."

"If there were any other way…"

"You could tell them the truth," he said. "If you dislike them so much, why do you care what they think?"

"I told you. I won't have them thinking less of Daddy."

"I'm not sure I'm following."

"I'm not asking you to," she whispered belligerently. "Just fold."

After they bundled the spread at the foot of the bed, she pulled back her corner of the covers and turned away to perch on the edge of the mattress. Noah watched her perform a demure striptease, untying her terry robe and slipping it gingerly off, one shoulder at a time. With a quick little lift of her hips she scooted it out from beneath her, then lay it over a bough that was part of the headboard.

She slid beneath the sheet and light blanket, gathered up the bed's three pillows and went about arranging them around her. One went under her stomach, another pressed to her back, the third under her head. Noah watched with what should have been totally clinical interest, but wasn't.

After her well-practiced pillow ballet, she settled beneath the covers, turning her back to him. "Good night, Noah," she murmured.

"Are you sure you have enough pillows?" he asked, amused.

"Plenty, thanks." She didn't look at him.

"Don't you want to put one between your knees?"

"I don't have another one."

"You could fold a towel—"

"I'm fine." She turned slightly to peer at him, her expression suddenly fretful. "Oh—I forgot about you."

"Gee, thanks," he teased.

She bit her lip. "I don't have another pillow." She fished at her back, and Noah could tell she was about to give up one of hers.

"Keep your pillows, Sally." He waved off her concern. "I don't sleep with one."

She hesitated for a moment, one arm still stretched around to her back. "You're sure?" she said.

"Absolutely."

"Okay—then, good night."

"Good night, Sally."

He remained standing on his side of the bed, watching as she turned away from him and settled down, clearly intent on sleep.

"Would it bother you if I read?"

She shifted to pass him a perturbed look. "Read?"

He indicated a book on the knotty pine bedside table. "I found it in the parlor bookshelf. Looks good and I'm a night person."

She shook her head. "Oh, fine. Now you tell me."

He couldn't help but smile. "Whose fault is it that your interview for a husband was inadequate?"

She turned away. "Next time I'll do better."

"Next time?" He grabbed a raspberry corduroy cushion off a chair at the vanity that stood beside the window, and propped it against the wrought-iron headboard.

"It's a figure of speech. If I'm lucky my grandparents won't be back."

He shook his head at her tartness, slipped into bed and lounged against the chair pad. "The light won't bother you?"

"Don't worry about me. I'm a heavy sleeper."

Noah switched on the lamp, feeling peculiarly restless. He wasn't sleepy and for some reason the book he'd thought would be interesting an hour ago had lost its appeal. Nevertheless he picked it up and flipped to chapter one. After a few pages, he faced the fact he was paying more attention to the sound of his bedmate's breathing than the grisly thriller.

Maybe he was antsy because he'd never shared a bed with a woman platonically before. The idea of being so near a horizontal female and doing *nothing* sexual was not an experience he'd had very often. To be accurate, it wasn't an experience he'd *ever* had. Not that he was a lustful, slavering beast where women were concerned. Even so, sleeping beside a lovely woman like Sally and acting as though she weren't there was difficult to pull off. Even…he checked the book jacket for the author's name. Even J. Everett Cranston, the "master of murder most foul," as the jacket certified, couldn't compete.

Her breathing was soft and regular. In one way he found the sound pleasant, in another, it aggravated the fire out of him. He certainly didn't intend to *do* anything sexual. There was Jane to consider. They'd been a steady couple for two years. Even so, Sally could at least have the decency to have a little trouble sleeping.

He went back to reading, but all too quickly it proved to be no diversion whatsoever. Aggravated with himself, he glanced at her. "I hope you don't snore," he said, unsure what incorrigible bit of brain matter had insisted on initiating a conversation. Especially with something so idiotic.

She didn't respond, and for some reason her silence affected him like a challenge. "I'm not a heavy sleeper myself," he added casually, eyeing her for signs of wakefulness.

She still didn't respond.

Damn. "Sally?" He was well aware any second now she'd turn over and clout him in the stomach, but that knowledge didn't blunt his unruly urge to provoke her. "Are you asleep?" Maybe it was the way her eyes shone when she was mad, or the peachy blush in her cheeks. Whatever it was making him stupid, it was going to earn him a fat lip.

"You'll know I'm asleep when I start snoring," she muttered. "Read your book."

He let loose with a chuckle and she shifted to look at him. "Why are you so jolly all of a sudden?"

He had no idea. "I thought I should warn you about my sensitivity to snoring," he kidded, but silently added, *I want to look at you. For some reason you make me feel—wired.*

He lay his book in his lap, quirking a brow as though to emphasize his snoring admonition.

She lay curled on her side, squinting at him like he was a bothersome gnat that kept buzzing in her ear. She'd plaited her hair in a short, single braid for sleeping. Wisps escaped all around her face, giving her a golden halo that was enticing and sexy. She heaved a weary sigh and turned away. "Thanks. Heaps."

He experienced a stab of annoyance at being turned on by a woman he'd only known for a few hours. Especially a woman on the very precipice of giving birth. He scanned her profile. Her skin was clear, her face scrubbed clean of any traces of makeup. Come to think of it, he didn't think she'd worn any makeup all day.

She looked seventeen, but she'd admitted to being a decade older, so he had to believe she was at least twenty-seven. The subtle scent of lavender soap wafted across the bed, an old-fashioned scent in an old-fashioned room of lace curtains, rough pine furniture and grandma's rag rugs. Not Grandma Vanderkellen's, but a good-old-down-home Texas grandma.

He liked Sally Johnson's bedroom, with its old-fangled feel of a turn-of-the-century farmhouse. Except the bed—that was modern. He scanned the iron footboard, made up of twining, leafy branches.

Noah found his gaze drawn to Sally's face, wondering if she was actually asleep or playing possum. Her white flannel gown was edged with a soft lace collar that had flipped up to mask the lower half of her face. For a moment he focused on her closed eyes. At least the one he could see from his seated position. Blond lashes fanned out across high cheekbones. He shifted his attention to her nose. It was slim and definitely aristocratic. Knowing her attitude about snobs, Noah felt sure she'd reject that analysis with high dudgeon.

She was a good-looking woman. It was hard for him to believe she was unattached. And, with her choice of such an antiseptic method of pregnancy—well, he was intrigued. She was old-fashioned in some ways, but her pregnancy was strictly space-age. She was outspoken and spunky, yet she seemed scared to death of her grandparents. She was beautiful and feminine, but she didn't want a man messing in her life. Being a card-carrying member of the male gender, to him her decision seemed like a tragic waste. For some reason he had to find out what made Sally Johnson tick.

Unable to keep a nagging question to himself any longer, he asked, "So, do you not like men, or what?"

She didn't react, so he leaned closer. "Sally?" He whispered her name, not wanting to wake her in case she really had fallen asleep. Without a good reason, he reached out and lifted the lace away from her face, gently smoothing it along her collarbone.

"What do you think you're doing?"

Noah was startled by her low-pitched, accusatory tone. She didn't sound the slightest bit sleepy. Shifting back to lounge against his pillow, he found himself fighting an undisciplined grin. "Just fixing your collar," he said, his tone as innocent as a newborn lamb. He wished his thoughts had been equally innocent. What was his problem, feeling randy and aroused? It was inappropriate and beneath contempt and he should be ashamed of himself.

"My collar was exactly the way I wanted it."

"So—" He cleared a wayward surge of mirth from his throat. "Do you want me to put it back?"

"No." She turned to glare at him. "And to answer your other question, I like men just fine—as long as they don't keep me awake asking questions that are none of their business." She glared a warning that a blood-bath would follow his next inquiry. "Satisfied?"

He nodded. "Check. Shut up, Noah."

Solemn-faced, she turned away.

"I'll read now," he said, amazed at his apparent intention to make a nuisance of himself. He was usually asleep before his head hit the pillow. Today, rounds at the hospital had begun at five. Why couldn't he leave her alone and go to sleep? "On second thought maybe we should get to know each other."

She heaved a theatrical sigh.

"Shouldn't you know a little about me?" he prodded. "Something might come up."

"I gave you your name, Dr. Step. I can wing anything that might come up."

He knew she could. But that wasn't really the point of this conversation. The real point was—hell if he knew! "What if Abigail asks me a question while you're out of the room, and you come in and blurt something inconsistent?"

"I'll try not to blurt." She peered at him. "Why are you so interested in getting our stories straight? Aren't you the one who was recommending truth a minute ago?"

"I'm fickle," he said, earning a scowl for his pestering.

"You're paying me back for making you miss your plane."

He sobered, the reminder of his ruined vacation plans and Jane's maneuverings coming back full force. "No," he shook his head. "That was totally my doing."

"Well?" she indicated the book. "I thought you were so hot for murder and mayhem."

He glanced at the book, wishing that was what he was

hot for. "Suddenly I'm not in the mood for murder," he murmured.

"How odd." She turned more on her back so she could better glare at him. "Suddenly I am."

Her blatant threat tickled him and he grinned. Why her spirited little retorts aroused him was a mystery, but *dammit,* they did. "What about our stories?"

She eyed the ceiling and turned fully to her back. "Okay." Smoothing the covers up to her chin, she peered at him. "You were born here in Houston."

"Wrong."

She closed her eyes as though counting to ten. "I'm *telling,* not asking."

"Oh." He lay the book aside. "I was born in Houston. What else?"

"You have an older brother and a younger sister."

"Why?"

She opened her eyes to frown at him, which only made his grin reappear. He was a little unsettled at how she seemed to have taken control of his ability to smile, a remarkable trick. He wondered how she pulled it off? "I don't know *why* you have an older brother and a younger sister," she said, sounding weary. "It's a cover."

"Why can't I be from where I'm from and be an only child, which I am?" He leaned toward her. "As a doctor, I can say without fear of contradiction that pregnancy does not dull the capacity to learn."

She closed her eyes, her expression pained. This time her count of ten took much longer. "Okay," she said at last. "If it'll shut you up, have it your way. Where were you born?"

He experienced a trace of ambivalence about revealing his connection with Boston, but decided the truth might help lessen her malice toward her grandparents. Once she got to know him, as a regular guy, she would understand Boston was full of friendly people—even some who had money and position. "I was born in Massachusetts."

She opened her eyes and met his gaze. "Really?"

He had her full attention. He liked having her full attention, but pretended nonchalance. "Somebody has to be from Massachusetts."

She rolled toward him, and came up on one elbow. "Where in Massachusetts?"

"A little burg of very little significance."

Her forehead knit. "Humor me."

"Okay. Maybe you've heard of it." His ambivalence resurfaced but he ignored it. "Boston?" he said.

All the years he'd lived in Texas, he'd never cared to enlighten people about his childhood and hometown, but for some reason, watching Sally Johnson's growing interest, or was it panic, he experienced an eerie regret that he started with her.

Her eyes narrowed with a look of startled wariness. "That's not true." She'd spoken quietly. Too quietly. "You talk like a Texan."

The deed was done. There was no going back. "I've lived in Texas since I was eighteen," he said. "When I decided to make Houston my home, I immersed myself in Texas 'tawk.'" He stretched and slowed his remark, exaggerating the Southwestern dialect for effect. "Like the 'fixin' to's, y'all's and the good-old-boy drawl." He shrugged, reverting to his normal cadence. "After all what kind of doctor would I be if I didn't understand a patient who complained she'd been 'in pine all die'?''

She swallowed, his little joke evidently making no impression. "Say something like a Bostonian," she said. "Through your nose."

He peered at her, disapprovingly. "That's not very flattering."

"It's not meant to be. If you're a Bostonian, you should be able to talk like one."

He'd purposely worked on losing his Boston-baked twang, but he figured if he put his mind to it, he could resurrect it. "Shoe-ah, whatevah," he began, feeling strangely as if he'd been exposed as a spy. "The killa bah on the peeah, jutting into the hahbah, serves hahd likkah, beah, chowdah, con on the cob, and a wicked lobstah with melted buttah—"

"Stop it!" she broke in, her expression wretched, as though she'd been betrayed. "That's enough! Oh—my—Lord…"

He could tell her brain was frantically processing what she considered was a horrible truth, and he wanted to kick himself. Why hadn't he just read the blasted book? "But—you're not one of *the* Boston Barretts, right?" Her question had the feel of a plea. "That's—not possible!"

As he'd guessed, little Miss I-Hate-Snobs may not have lived in Boston, but she was well aware of its hierarchy of blue-bloods.

The truth about his heritage would do their storytelling no good. Maybe he should have waited to break the news to her. He definitely should have waited. This was too much, too soon. "Never mind." He shook his head, regretfully. "You're right. Dr. Step needs to be born and bred in Houston."

She stared, mute and miserable.

He felt like a jerk. What had that exercise accomplished besides making his presence more abhorrent to her than before? Obviously when he decided to tell her about his Boston background, he hadn't been thinking with the brain, *above* his waist. "What do you say?" he asked, trying to repair an irreparable rift. "Dr. Tommy Noah Step is from Houston. Let's say we met at—" He stopped. "Where did we meet?"

She opened her mouth, then closed it.

He tried to move the topic away from his hometown and her least favorite subject matter. Boston Snobs. "It can't be school," he went on, "since I'm thirty-five. What about a blind date?"

"But—in Boston, there's a saying. What is it?" she whispered, clearly not listening. "'The Vanderkellens bow only to the Barretts, and the Barretts bow only to God.' You're not one of *those* Barretts?"

If some wayward unconscious objective in all this had been another look into her wide, silver gaze, he'd done a blasted perfect job. From the liquid shimmer in those big eyes, he feared another few seconds would bring with it a torrent of tears.

He cursed himself for being an insensitive bum. Why hadn't he let her go to sleep? Didn't she have enough to contend with? He had no idea she'd ever heard that ridiculous adage or he would never have brought it up. "Forget it." He waved off the subject. "I'm a Houston Barrett, now. I hardly ever get back."

She jerked up to sit, clutching the bedcovers to her

breast. "You *are!* You *are* one of the Boston Barretts!" She ran a trembly hand through her hair, blond wisps fluttering and dancing in a tempting display. "So—so if that's really true, why didn't my grandparents recognize you?"

He shrugged. "Hubert almost did. But it's been years since I've—"

"Oh—that's just great!" she cried. "I knew you were a bighead, but I didn't know you were the prince of bigheads!"

That made him angry, but not with her. He should have kept his parentage a deep, dark secret. Why did he think knowing he was a Boston Barrett would ease her hostility of Boston society? He'd always thought he was pretty down-to-earth, but according to his sham-wife, he had a thoroughly distorted opinion of himself. "Bighead?" he repeated, his ego pricked. "Give me a break. I express a medical opinion about single motherhood and suddenly I'm the prince of bigheads?"

She pulled her knees up as close as she could and hugged them, curling herself into a protective ball. "My mother told me about the Barretts." She stared into space, going pale.

He couldn't believe how badly she was taking such *nothing* news. Scowling at her ashen profile, he gritted out, "Good Lord, Sally, my grandfather is Morris Barrett, a banker, not Vlad the Impaler."

She glanced his way, eyes bright with unshed tears. "Did it give you a good laugh—watching me slam Boston snobs, when all the time..." A tear trembled on her lower lashes, lost its hold and skimmed down her cheek. Noah watched its journey with growing self-disgust.

He gritted his teeth. "Considering who my family is, I thought it was ironic—okay…" he amended through a tired exhale. The truth couldn't make her loathe him more thoroughly "…and maybe a little amusing."

"A little amusing!" she repeated through clamped jaws. With a flash of defensive spirit, she turned on him. "For your information, Dr. Blue-Blood Barrett, I never lived in Boston, so the fact that I'm a Vanderkellen and you're a high-and-mighty Barrett means nothing to me. I don't bow to you nor to anybody! Understood?" Her eyes sparked with bitter hostility. It was a spectacular sight, and Noah had the wildest, out-of-character urge to drag her into his arms. Which was, no doubt, the *stupidest* idea he'd had in an hour filled with whopping stupid ideas.

"Hell!" he blew the word through clenched teeth, damning himself for the way his light teasing and misguided good intentions had gone so awry. "I was just—"

"Laughing at me," she cut in. "I know!"

"That's not what I was going to say."

"I don't care what you were going to say," she shot back, struggling from the bed and grabbing her robe.

"What are you doing?"

She shoved her arms into the sleeves and tied the sash without responding.

"Sally?" He slid from the bed. "Where do you think you're going?"

"I'm going to sleep on the glider on the back porch."

"Oh, no, you're not." He caught up with her at the

door and slapped the flat of his hand against it. "You're not going anywhere."

She tugged on the doorknob but the pressure of his hand against the wood made her efforts fruitless. "Leave me alone!" she cried, tugging on the door as she tried to shoulder him aside. "I sleep on the porch a lot on mild nights."

"Not while I'm your husband."

She shoved against his chest with her shoulder. "Don't get carried away with the part. The show closes in a couple of days."

"It closes tonight if you leave this room," he said, astonished at how vehemently opposed he was to having her walk out.

She stopped grappling and stared up at his face. "You mean you'd leave?"

"Like a tree in springtime." It was a bad play on words, but he was in no mood to be profound. He didn't like the idea of heading to Aruba and Jane quite yet, but he would leave, go back to his apartment, and let Sally deal with her grandparents' belittling any way she could.

He made sure his silence and intimidating expression left no doubt about whose problem this was and who was doing her a favor by being there.

Though her features remained belligerent, she swallowed hard. Their staring war went on for several tense seconds before she broke eye contact. At the same time her fist dropped from the doorknob.

"Okay, you win." Blinking back tears she faced him, head unbowed. "I'll stay, but I won't like it."

He had to give her credit. She had spirit.

The sight of her glaring at him, her lower lip trem-

bling, made his gut tighten with compassion and something else—something bothersome and undeniable. He
suddenly felt buoyant and crooked a wry grin. "Don't
look so miserable. We're a good team." Squeezing her
shoulders in an encouraging way, he winked. "The
Prince of Bigheads and Princess Bountiful."

Without analyzing why, he lowered his head and
grazed her lips with his, experiencing the delicate tremble of her mouth. The infinitesimal tremor affected him
deeply.

On their own, his hands did a slow slide from her
shoulders, his fingers spreading across her back. His
arms, on their own, pressed her gently against him. His
lips caressed hers, arresting their trembling. Though his
kiss was meant to be perfunctory, a whisper-light reas-
surance, Noah found himself lingering. The soft, moist
taste of her lips sparked a restless hunger deep inside
him. He felt suddenly full of adrenaline, very alive. The
pure, naked gratification of the experience was shocking.

Noah was in big trouble.

CHAPTER FIVE

WHEN Noah's lips met Sally's, she was stunned into a state of suspended animation. She couldn't move, couldn't think, beyond the realization that his mouth was moving slowly, seductively across hers, leaving in his wake a trail of fire. The kiss was light as kisses went, but the caress of his mouth produced a sweet throbbing in her lips, and a soft sigh issued up from her throat.

His kiss was exquisitely tender, yet the contact was provocative and wildly masculine, drugging her brain and her limbs. Any fleeting thought of resistance was obliterated in the breathless wonder of it all. Sally had been kissed before, but never like this. Never had a mere meeting of lips occasioned a deep, aching hunger in her. She felt a searing desire to fully discover the pleasure and promise foreshadowed in Noah's kiss.

As the powerful need coursed through her, the ability to move returned to her paralyzed limbs. Sliding her arms around him, she spread her hands on his skin, exploring, delighting in his male texture. She breathed in his scent, welcoming the light, aromatic tang of soap that clung to him. He was clean and warm and exquisitely male. She loved the tingle of his vital heat beneath her fingertips. It had been too long since she'd known the touch or kiss of a man.

Her breakup with her fiancé...how long had it been? Nearly two years? She hadn't realized until now how detached she'd felt, not until Noah's lips met hers, and his hands, hot and seductive on her back, began their tantalizing quest down the curve of her spine.

Her body thrummed with urgency, yearned to be conquered, her passion primitive and explosive.

Pressed to him as she was, his body fairly burned hers. She could feel the thud of his heartbeat and trembled with anticipation as his tongue nudged her lips. She surrendered to his primal solicitation with impetuous abandon, rejoicing as his tongue paid hot, sweet tribute to the inner frontier of her mouth.

One of his hands slipped down to cup her hip, fanning the flames of her arousal. Her body glowed, her heart raced, hammering in her chest.

Something else within her hammered, too. Painfully. She winced. Noah let out a low grunt, his lips lifting to hover above hers. "What in blazes...?" he muttered hoarsely.

Sally was slow to fall back to reality. Though his hands lingered on her, she sensed that some unseen director had shouted "Cut" to their impromptu love scene. Just in time, if the lust rampaging through her body was any indication. Experiencing an unpalatable jumble of dejection and reprieve, she dragged her arms from Noah's back and stumbled a step away.

His brows knit and he stared at her. Rather, at her stomach. "Your little Vivica kicked the hell out of me." He met Sally's gaze, his expression troubled and apologetic. "She was right. I deserved it." She watched as his jaw muscles jerked. The self-accusing downturn of his lips drew her gaze, warming her blood. Even his frown was sexy. The sight was more than Sally could deal with at the moment. She was having enough trouble catching her breath.

Lowering her gaze to his chest—*wrong*—his shorts—*definitely, wrong*—to his bare feet, she placed her hands on her belly. Vivica was kicking up a storm, the little busybody. *No, no! That kick was a good thing!* her rational side argued. *You have no business rolling around steaming up windows with this man. First, you'd probably bring on early labor, and second, you only met the guy today!*

Reckless sexual behavior was absolutely foreign to Sally's nature. She couldn't imagine what came over her. She swallowed hard several times, but she failed to dislodge the wad of mortification wedged in her throat.

"Now..." She stopped then swallowed again in an attempt to overcome the shaky warble. "Now, will you let me sleep on the glider?" She couldn't look him in the eyes. How could she have allowed things to go that far?

"Sally," he said her name softly, gently squeezing her upper arms. "I won't attack you again. Besides, I saw that glider. It's skinny and the padding is thin. There's no reason for you to have to sleep on something that uncomfortable, especially in your condition. I'll be good."

I have no doubt! a rude imp in her brain taunted. *You've already been spectacular!*

She rubbed her eyes, working to get her emotions under control. She sensed sincerity in his words and his brief, encouraging touch, and was sure he hadn't meant anything indecent by the remark. And his comment about the glider was true. As pregnant as she was, it wasn't the best choice for bedding. With a reluctant nod, she agreed and turned away. "Good night."

Her fingers trembling, she untied her sash and slipped out of the robe, draping it over the wrought-iron footboard. Without chancing a peek at Noah, she slipped beneath the covers and arranged the pillows around her. Only after she was settled in did she hear the creak of a floorboard, indicating that Noah had moved.

She squeezed her eyes tight. It would be safer if she didn't chance seeing the body she'd all but surrendered to. *Would have surrendered to,* if not for little Vivica's prenatal vigilance. She placed a protective hand on the baby, now peaceful. Sally only wished her own emotions were as serene.

She heard the squeak of bedsprings and gasped, then realized how idiotic that was. Noah was merely slipping into bed.

"Would you rather I didn't?"

Sally could tell from the location of his voice that he'd paused, half in and half out. Inwardly she said, *I would rather you were the skinny orderly I'd expected to show up. Then we'd have no problem!* Instead she shook her head. "No. Just—just keep to your side."

A pause. "I've never done anything like that before."

"What?" she asked, flustered. "Kept to your side?"

"No, I meant—the kiss. I've never jumped a patient like that before."

"I'm not a patient," she murmured, not quite sure what her point was.

He exhaled long and low, sounding tired. "If you were, I'd be explaining my behavior to the Medical Ethics Board."

She experienced a crazy, sympathetic twinge. "Forget it," she said. "It was as much my fault as yours. I—I've been—well, alone for a long time. So, maybe—" She stopped herself, horrified she'd admitted that out loud. Wishing she could disappear, she made a pained face. "I don't want to talk about it anymore, Doctor," she whispered. "I need to get up early."

"I understand. No problem."

The bed squawked and bobbed as he got in. After another few heartbeats the bedside light went out, surprising her. "Don't you want to read?"

"Not even a little bit," he muttered.

Noah woke to the sound of banging. Though he was no expert, metal hitting metal would be his guess. He looked toward the window. Faint, orange fingers of light filtered through the lacy curtain, hinting at a dawning day. Out there, very close by, some poor, defenseless piece of metal was being violently beaten into submission. He hoped it wasn't his truck.

Groggy from a night without much sleep, he dropped his legs over the side of the bed and sat up. He rubbed his bleary eyes and ran both hands through his hair trying to get his brain working. The banging ceased and he blew out a weary breath. That was good, but the silence came too late. Sleeping—rather lying very still while wide-awake—next to Sally Johnson, was not his idea of rest.

He glanced over his shoulder, experiencing a surge of guilt for watching her sleep. To his surprise she wasn't there. He stood up, frowning at the spot where she'd peacefully slept for too many hours he could vividly remember. He'd wiled away those hours counting her slow, even breaths.

The banging began again and he straightened, alert. "What in blazes is that?" he asked the empty space. Was there a foundry somewhere in the surrounding piney woods he hadn't noticed? No wonder Sally got up early. Who could sleep with that racket going on?

He grabbed a pair of jeans from the suitcase he'd stuffed into Sally's closet, yanked them on and padded from the room, intent on finding the source of the clamor.

As he reached the Vanderkellens's room, Abigail stuck her head out the door. "Good, you're going to stop her."

Noah halted, assuming he'd heard wrong, since what she said made little sense. "Good morning, Grandmother Vanderkellen." He gave her a grandson-in-law-bright smile he didn't feel. "What did you say?"

She stuck a hand outside the narrow opening and wagged blue-veined fingers. "I said, I'm relieved to see you're going to make Sally stop that infernal noise. There is no excuse for her to be welding in the middle of the night!"

Welding? Sally? The image of the pretty, pregnant blonde being the source of such a crashing cacophony didn't even compute. Besides, if that noise was welding, somebody wasn't doing it right.

Since he was playing Sally's deliriously happy husband, he decided not to argue the point before he found out what was going on. He retained his grin. "Noise?" He shrugged. "I didn't notice." Her aghast expression was priceless. "I was going to take her a cup of coffee," he improvised. "Would you care for some?"

She looked as riled as he'd ever seen her. "I suppose, since I can't sleep with all that..." She wagged again. "This is no way to treat guests! Apparently such discourteous behavior is acceptable in Texas!" Abigail slammed the door before Noah could respond, which was for the best.

Annoyed, he muttered, "So is getting your attitude adjusted with a whop upside the head." The more he was around that woman the more he leaned toward Sally's side of the argument, even if he couldn't make much sense of it. One thing was obvious. There was precious little evidence of familial sentimentality among the Vanderkellens.

He took the stairs two at a time. The rapid-paced explosions of sound pulled him out the back door, through the screened porch, across a yard dotted with tall, skinny pines, to a half-hidden barn. The structure was weathered and windowless with a galvanized sheet steel roof; its double-doored entry was closed. But even shut up as it was, the bashing sound rang discordantly in the crisp air. *Clang-clang-clang-clang.* The piercing beat seemed to pump bursts of light into a day that became more and more discernible with every boom. Noah realized that was an irrational thought, but he hadn't had much sleep.

Even as he cracked the door open, he couldn't picture Sally Johnson as a welder. A clog dancer, perhaps. A political activist, yes. Even the lead trumpet for a jazz-funk band. But a welder? Not in a million years.

Aged rafters were ghostly and indistinct above the dim light provided by two utilitarian fixtures, each containing one, low-wattage bulb. He scanned the interior, transformed from a cow barn into what looked like a blacksmith shop.

His gaze trailed over orderly racks of hammers and tongs, two band saws and a couple of anvils. Chained to a cart, between massive steel worktables, were several acetylene tanks. A bright yellow, freestanding crane towered, like an armor-plated tyrannosaurus rex, dwarfing everything else in the studio. A hooded forge yawned, scattering cinders from the red-hot conflagration blazing in its throat.

Amid the steel and fire, Sally looked small and vulnerable. She stood with her back to him. From what he could see, she was dressed in overalls. On top of that she wore a heavy leather apron, leather gloves, a short, hide jacket and a red baseball cap, its brim at her nape. Ear protectors, like high-tech earmuffs, safeguarded her from going deaf, and goggles shielded her eyes.

With the poise of a lion tamer, she stood before the iron monster doing the deafening pounding and gnashing. The trip-hammer chewed and flattened a cherry-red metal rod as she gradually, unflinchingly drew it from the beast's jaws.

Noah walked inside and the heat hit him in the face. The air was hot and sultry; its smell reminded him of an old-fashioned, coal-burning steam train. He wondered what the place must be like in the dead of a Texas summer. Lounging against a long, steel table strewn with equipment he could only guess at, he found himself a little in awe of this astonishing woman. One thing was sure. She wasn't welding. She was creating.

Now that the mystery was solved, he glanced around.

Against one rough-hewn wall leaned what looked like half of a gate, formed in the likeness of a butterfly's wing. He was impressed by the way solid metal had been transformed into airy shapes of such delicate fluidity.

He shook his head. So Sally was a metal artist. Did Abigail *not* know the difference between being an artist and a welder? Was she such a snob she thought anybody who worked with their hands was beneath notice? Ridiculous! *Doctors* work with their hands.

He hadn't given any thought to what Sally might do to earn her living. But if he had, it wouldn't have been this—a pleasant surprise. As he scanned the studio, he caught sight of a bookcase in one corner that contained trophies. Were they hers? If so, why were they out in the barn instead of inside?

The woman was turning out to be quite an enigma. A fetching, spirited, talented and frustrating enigma. Shoving away from the table, he decided he might as well go shower and change and fix Abigail's coffee. He could ask his questions later, when it didn't require shouting or setting his clothes on fire.

Sally came inside, surprised to find Noah lounging at the kitchen table. He looked—good, sitting there. Too good, in the chest-hugging knit shirt and faded jeans. She would have to ask him one day how a doctor got so dratted muscular. What did he do, bench-press his patients?

Instinctively she swiped the damp hair out of her face. "Oh—hi." She wiped sweaty hands on her overalls. "I didn't expect you'd be up."

He sat back from the table, looking skeptical. "You

didn't think that pounding machine of an alarm clock would rouse me? If there's a cemetery anywhere around, you've got a horror movie's worth of angry, wakeful dead on their way here.'' He took up his mug and sipped.

"Oh..." She felt badly. "I don't usually have guests. Did the noise wake—''

"Not Hubert. Those pills knocked him out. But Abigail...'' He lifted an eyebrow and let the sentence fade.

Sally made a contrite face. "I'm sure she was delighted. She hates to be reminded her granddaughter is 'a welder.'''

Noah sat down his mug. "She mentioned the welding.'' He motioned toward the table. "Have some coffee and sit.''

"I need to shower.''

"Take a minute.'' He pushed up and went to the cupboard where the mugs were stored, took one down and filled it with steaming coffee. "It's the gourmet stuff Abigail insisted I buy.'' He set it at the chair around the corner from his. "I figure that diamond-studded watch of hers is worth twenty-five thousand. She can afford to let us drink some of her decaf Colombian-Mocha.'' He held out a hand, taking her fingers and guiding her to the chair. "Strike a blow for welders everywhere.'' His wink was taunting and sarcastic, she was sure, but even so the effect was frighteningly sensual. Sally's legs turned to mush. For Vivica's sake, she sank into the chair.

She took the mug between her fingers. How strangely cold her hands felt against the hot mug, especially considering where she'd just been and the near molten metal she'd been working. Even her elk-skin gloves weren't enough to ward off the intense heat. "I'm not a welder," she said, looking into the mug. Its rich, mocha-tinged aroma wafted up with the steam.

"I know that."

She glanced up, startled. "How?"

He took his seat and indicated the direction of the barn with a nod. "I went out there. It's obvious you're an artist." His brows knit as he seemed to have a thought. "Did you design our bed?"

Our bed? His use of the word "our" did something unruly to her insides. If he only knew how rough a night she'd spent, sharing that bed with him. She'd tried to sleep but spent most of the night pretending to. Breathing regularly, slowly. It was ironic, that she'd never worked so hard in her life trying to sound utterly relaxed.

When she'd slept at all, she'd had the most brazenly lewd dreams—and Noah Barrett played a brazenly lewd part. Pushing the lush memories back, she tried to refocus on the conversation. He'd asked about what? Oh, the bed. She nodded. "It was commissioned by an engaged couple who split up on their honeymoon. They'd paid half up-front, but reneged on the rest, so I decided to keep it rather than try to sell it to somebody else."

He pursed his lips, his gaze intent, that light, sexy blue reminiscent of those too-erotic dreams. "It's a fine piece of work," he said.

Heat crawled up her cheeks. A compliment and those seductive eyes was a hard combination to deal with.

"Thanks," she whispered, chagrined to hear how weak her voice had become.

"What else do you do?"

She gathered herself together and cleared her throat. "My work is mainly custom. Gates, stair banisters, garden benches. Functional, one-of-a-kind sculptural things."

"What were you working on this morning?"

She took a stalling sip of her coffee and was startled by how delicious it was. "This is good," she murmured.

"Thanks."

She glanced at him. "Oh? The taste is solely due to your superior coffeemaking talent?"

His lips twisted in a sardonic grin that was entirely unfair. "Compliments won't get the subject changed."

She blinked, momentarily befuddled, before recalling he'd asked what she was working on. "Oh, right. It's Vivica's cradle. I had to finish a commissioned piece before I could start on it." She rubbed her shoulder where a muscle complained. She'd laid so stiffly last night, never daring to turn over, she had a cramp that wouldn't go away. "It's coming along. I should have it finished before Vivica's birthday."

"I didn't notice anything that looked like a cradle."

She sipped again then set her mug down. "How flattering."

He was silent for a long moment. His gaze trained on her made her nervous. At last, he moved, taking a drink from the mug he'd been holding, then set it down. "I'll look around more thoroughly next time."

"Don't bother."

He arched a questioning brow and looked as if he was

going to respond, then closed his mouth, seeming to decide to let the peevish remark go. For some reason that irked her. "I know what you're thinking," she charged.

"Really?" he asked.

"You're thinking, 'I'll let her cantankerous sniping go because she's very pregnant and uncomfortable and that's making her cranky.' Well, don't do me any favors. My pregnancy doesn't have a thing to do with my attitude." She dared him with her eyes. "That *is* what you were thinking, right?"

He sat forward, relaxing his forearms on the table. "Actually I was thinking I'd let the crabby smart-mouthing go, but cantankerous sniping is good, too."

"Crabby smart-mouthing!" she echoed, a new surge of irritation washing over her. Why did his candor upset her? Didn't she ask for it?

"So, you make a living at your art?"

Startled by the casual remark, she glared at him, her expression pinched. "That's a pretty personal question."

"I'm your husband, remember?" He indicated the second floor. "What if they ask?"

"They won't. They'll assume my rich doctor-husband supports me."

"Don't you want them to know your artistic talent earns you a living? Not many artists can say that, or the term 'starving artist' wouldn't be such a cliché."

"I don't care what they think."

"Like hell you don't," he said, his tone low and challenging. "Why go through with this farce if you don't care?"

She shrugged. Of course, he wouldn't understand. "It's complicated."

"Contradictions in behavior usually are."

She felt the stab of his cynicism and passed him a sharp look. "Make up your mind. Are you an obstetrician or a psychiatrist?"

He watched her for a heartbeat. "Make up *your* mind." He spoke quietly, but his words held the daunting edge of an indictment. "Do you care what they think or don't you?"

She didn't like the way this coffee break was going. "I told you it's complicated. I don't want to discuss it." She struggled to her feet. "I'm going to take a shower. While I'm gone, why don't you practice keeping your nose out of my business!"

She felt a hand on her arm. "Look, Sally," he said, halting her escape. "It's not good for you—or the baby—to be tense and angry all the time." He moved around to face her, forcing her to make eye contact. "Ease up. Give yourself a break."

"You give *me* a break." She yanked on his hold but he didn't let her go. "You *doctors*. You think you have all the answers! If you'd quit prying into my personal life, I'd be as calm as—as *calm!*" She lifted her chin, annoyed at herself for being so fuzzy-headed. Evidently lack of sleep was making her stupid as well as snappish.

"Well, at least tell me when we got married," he groused. "I deserve to know that."

His request took her by surprise. She'd never even thought about it. "I don't know. Sometime before I got pregnant."

"Last May?"

"Make it April."

"April what?"

"Pick a day. I don't care."

"The first."

She shot him a disgruntled look. "Why April Fool's Day?"

"It feels right," he muttered. "I've never felt so much like the butt of a joke in my life."

His chide stung. He had a point. He was doing her a whopping big favor, and she was repaying him by acting like a spoiled, stubborn shrew. It was just that she'd kept her feelings and resentments, her hopes and dreams, locked up inside so long, even the idea of sharing them caused her physical pain.

If the whole truth were told, even Sam didn't fully understand her burning resentment toward their grandparents. He'd visited them several times since their mother died, and made his peace. But, then, Sam was an almighty physician. Clearly he'd been the one sibling to inherit the dominant and superior Vanderkellen genes, while she, *the welder,* had been stocked with every last inferior, blue-collar *Johnson* characteristic. Her stomach clenched with revulsion for such prejudicial reasoning. Her father had been a heroic man, a firefighter, who'd lost his life saving others. How dare they…

Vivica kicked, startling Sally out of her musings, and she realized she'd been holding her breath. Her anger and resentment was so overpowering, so focused, she could have passed out! *Good Lord,* Noah was right. She was too angry, too tense. It wasn't good for her baby.

She lifted her gaze to meet Noah's. He was frowning. She rubbed her stomach where Vivica's little foot or elbow lingered, poking. After a long, hard-fought internal battle, she nodded. "Okay, you're right. You deserve to know some things.'' Indicating the table she said, ''Drink your coffee. I'll talk.''

He didn't immediately react, so she tugged on his hold to reiterate her desire that he release her. The warmth of his touch was too redolent of…well, recollections she was better off not recollecting.

When he let her go, he gathered up their mugs and refilled them before taking his seat. When he did, he met her gaze, his eyes vivid. ''Well?''

She was having nagging second thoughts. For so many years she'd been deeply bitter about her grandparents' abandonment of their only child because she'd run away to marry a Texas firefighter. Now that they were elderly, they were feeling the pinch of isolation that their selfish cruelty had caused. Did they expect her to welcome them with open arms? Well, she couldn't. She couldn't even talk about it. Not yet.

Still, she owed Noah something for all he was doing for her. With a heavy heart and leaden feet, she moved to the table and sat down. ''I'll answer the question about why I got pregnant,'' she said, soul-weary and irritated that he'd managed to coerce even this concession. ''That'll have to satisfy your curiosity. Agreed?''

His silent, grim scrutiny was her only answer.

CHAPTER SIX

SALLY stared him down. Dr. Noah Barrett wasn't going to make her feel guilty for keeping painful feelings to herself. "Agreed?" she repeated, making it clear she was not flexible on the subject.

He sat back. "Okay," he growled, crossing his arms over his chest. "It's a start."

She didn't like the sound of that. Evidently he planned to have her spill her guts before he left on vacation. Well, he was welcome to live in his little fantasy world. Doctors and their *I know what's best for you* attitude made her want to scream.

Noah cleared his throat as if to suggest she was not, yet, saying anything. She grabbed her coffee cup in both hands and took a swig. It burned all the way down and she made a face.

"Don't gulp it," he said, drawing her glare.

"Don't tell me what to do!" She slammed down the mug. "I'll do as I please, *when* I please. I'm an adult, and I don't have to kowtow to any bigheaded, pompous, stuffed shirt of a *doctor* or his high-handed, condescending orders!"

Noah looked annoyed by her outburst. "The coffee's very hot. Do you really want to burn your mouth?" he asked, plainly ticked off by her disproportionate outrage.

She felt a stab of remorse for biting off his head. She wasn't usually such a shrew. Until this second, she hadn't faced the fact she was still smarting badly from her breakup with her fiancé. After all, Noah wasn't Wayne—*Dr. Wayne Post*—who had made it clear that a cardiologist's wife was *not* supposed to have callused hands. And she should *not* spend all day sweating over a blacksmith's forge, hammering metal into "fence pieces and stair rails." A cardiologist's wife had to be ladylike and sophisticated and belong to all the right society leagues.

When she'd laughed, calling such notions foolishness, he'd dumped her flat.

Unfortunately Noah was not only a doctor but a Boston Barrett, too. All his life the man had been accustomed to people, more sophisticated with hands much less callused than hers, being thrilled to bow, scrape and cater to his whims. She looked down at her palms, roughened from the hard, hot work they did.

"Sally?" Noah asked. "Are you in there?"

His question drew her sharp glare. Feeling oddly caught in the act, she dropped her hands to her lap. When she met his gaze, she was startled by a note of compassion in his expression.

"Is something wrong with your hands?" he asked.

"Not a thing," she snapped.

He looked puzzled, as though he couldn't imagine why his concern would anger her. Could she blame him for his confusion? "It's nothing," she muttered. "I just—for a second you reminded me of my ex-fiancé."

He pursed his lips as though absorbing the revelation. "Your ex-fiancé?"

"Yes." She didn't like his pessimistic tone. "Why? Didn't you think I could get a man to propose to me?"

His jaws clinched. She could tell by the way the muscles bunched. "I thought a lot of things, but that wasn't one of them." He eyed his mug for a minute, then lifted his gaze to recapture hers. "I gather the breakup wasn't amicable."

She ground her teeth. "He was a doctor, like you. He also had the obnoxious habit of telling me how to run my life. You might as well know, I don't take orders well."

Noah's brows lifted. "Sweetheart," he said, his tone sardonic. "I can't see myself ever taking your ex's side, but you might as well know, you don't take orders *at all.*" He picked up his mug and sipped, watching her over the rim as he drank. His penetrating stare had an amazing power to ensnare and bewitch. Sally couldn't turn away, no matter how hard she tried.

When he lowered his mug to the table, he lifted his head in a half nod, as if to say, *I'm listening.*

She was prepared to get up and leave, but something in his expression held her. She'd expected overbearing insolence, looked for it, yet his expression didn't smack of a desire to dominate or demand. What she saw in his face, in his relaxed demeanor, was more receptive than she would have imagined. Or maybe it was simply that doctors who dealt on a day-to-day basis with emotional, pregnant women learned sneakier ways to manipulate.

No matter which was true, she'd promised to tell him about the artificial insemination. Oddly her ire had receded slightly and she felt a pang of guilt for snapping at him. Okay, so he was a doctor *and* a Barrett. Even so, it was unfair to stereotype him. That was the way her grandparents had behaved toward her father. Was she no better than they? She inhaled for courage. "Well, I—I decided to get pregnant this way because I love kids."

"You told me that much, yesterday."

She frowned. "Oh? Okay." She started to speak. Unable to form words, she paused to regroup. "Okay— it's because generations of women in my family have had—female problems. My mother had to have a hysterectomy at twenty-nine, and she told me her mother…" Sally indicated the upstairs. "Grandmother, had the same problem. Grandmother's older sister did, too. Only one great-aunt didn't need a hysterectomy by thirty, so I figured my odds weren't good. If my baby-making days are numbered, I'd better get started." She spoke with intentional firmness. "You see? My reason is completely logical."

He didn't speak. His serious expression didn't ease. Finally, he asked, "What, exactly, is the medical problem?"

She supposed she knew he would ask. With a shrug, she broke eye contact. "Fibroid tumors. The women in my family get them more rapidly and earlier than most."

"Have you been diagnosed with them?"

She felt as if she'd been transported into a doctor's examining room. "Are you charging for this consultation?" she asked, not even trying to hide her aggravation. The fact that she hadn't been diagnosed with fibroid tumors, yet, didn't help her argument, so she kept that to herself. "Funny, I don't remember making an appointment."

"I'm trying to get a clear picture of—"

"The *clear* picture I'm attempting to give you is the

soundness of my reason for choosing artificial insemination. Besides, I didn't promise you a discussion and I didn't ask for medical advice. I simply said I'd give you an explanation. I've done that. I'm pregnant. I'm happy and I'm not asking you to condone it.''

''No, you're asking me to help cover it up.''

Though his accusation was soft-spoken, it stung like a slap. She opened her mouth to retort, but something kept her from speaking. A little voice in her head jeered, *Just because his remark hurts doesn't make it any less true.* She dropped her gaze to her lap to watch her hands curl into fists of frustration.

''I hope you really are happy,'' he said.

She peered at him. ''What is that supposed to mean?''

He placed a forearm on the table, leaning toward her. ''It means, being a parent is tough duty. Tougher if you're the only parent.''

''You think I don't know that?'' she charged. ''Do you actually believe I didn't think long and hard before I made this decision?''

''I hope you did.''

His dubious tone threw fuel on her smoldering belligerence, and it flared to life. ''This is *great!*'' She struggled up from her chair, glaring at him. ''Upstairs I have a pair of condescending snobs and down here, a condescending *bore!* Which to choose?'' She struck a pose. Pressing the back of her hand to her forehead, she pretended to be caught up in a dreadful quandary. *''Which to choose?''*

A beat later, she tossed him a go-to-blazes scowl. ''How strange. It wasn't a tough choice after all.'' To emphasize her hostile withdrawal, she presented him with her ramrod-stiff back and stomped off.

Exactly twenty-four hours later, Abigail graced them with her presence in the kitchen. Apparently she decided germs and varmints were preferable to Hubert's wakeful moans and slumbering snores. Before Abigail would venture out, it had taken Noah's assurances that the Vanderkellens's granddaughter was a clean freak. That fact grated on Sally's nerves. As if she didn't already have *enough* grating on them. She felt like a slab of cheddar.

She had half a mind to hire a few cockroaches to skitter across the breakfast table, simply to get her grandmother's goat. But, of course, she would never do such a thing. Not even to a cockroach. After all, she was her mother's daughter, and Vivica had been a stickler for cleanliness. Meeting Abigail, Sally could see where she got it, though her mother hadn't been paranoid on the subject. Still, Sally knew how to scrub and disinfect with the best of the clean freaks.

Her clean-freakiness aside, it was clear she had not inherited her mother's charm, at least not to the extent of Noah's talent in that area. After Mrs. Vanderkellen had been at the kitchen table for barely ten minutes, Sally witnessed a miracle. Abigail's eternally puckered mouth actually spread in a smile. *Briefly,* but it had been there.

Still chafing at Noah's unsupportive attitude about her pregnancy, Sally took a seat across the table from him. They'd hardly spoken yesterday, and though he'd slipped into her bed last night, he'd done so without a word. Sally had found two more pillows in a cedar chest and built a mighty fortification around herself, so it was questionable whether he'd detected her. If he did, he'd plainly lost the urge to talk to her. Worst of all was the fact that, even safe behind her feathery fortress, she hadn't slept any better than the night before.

She yawned.

"Sleepy, sugarplum?"

Startled to be included in the conversation, she shot Noah a look. Abruptly closing her mouth, she shook her head. "No—I'm fine."

He smiled, and it looked genuinely loving. If the doctoring business ever went bust, he could make it as an actor. "You're sure?" he asked.

She held her temper, but only by a thread, and smiled back. "Of course, why do you ask?"

He indicated Abigail. "Grandmother asked you a question."

She blinked, surprised, and stifled another yawn. "Uh—what, Grandmother?"

Abigail tapped a jewelry-heavy finger on yesterday's mail, lying on the tabletop. "I asked you why you aren't using your husband's name? Why is the mail coming to Sally Johnson? Haven't you been married for a year?"

Sally experienced a tingle of alarm. Why hadn't she thought of the mail? Her habit of leaving it out on the kitchen table, to pay bills or answer letters, had caught her in her lie. "Oh—I…" She cast a panicky glance at Noah. He seemed as interested in her answer as Abigail.

Help me! she cried telepathically. "I—uh…" She looked at her grandmother, the wheels in her head spinning, making a whirring sound in her ears. Not much help. When would she learn if she was going to lie she would have to get better at it.

The scrape of a chair being shoved away from the table caught her attention. Noah was coming to his feet. "Not quite a year, Grandmother," Noah said, with a smile aimed at Sally that hinted of "I told you so." "April 1st is our anniversary." He moved around the table. "You see, darling? I told you there would be complications."

Told her? Complications? She was confused, and confusion didn't help her thought processes one bit.

"Grandmother, dear," he went on, patting Abigail's shoulder as he passed behind her. "Sugarplum decided to keep her name for professional reasons."

"Professional reasons?" Abigail echoed, her tone disapproving. The pinched quality returned to her mouth as she eyed her granddaughter. Sally could almost hear her thinking, *Welding is hardly a profession!* After a grim pause, Abigail barked, "Poppycock!"

"I believe that was my exact word." Noah's crooked grin caused a distressing increase in Sally's heart rate. "Poppycock," he repeated, a roguish twinkle in his eye. What was on the man's mind? If he thought he was helping, he was going about it in a convoluted way.

As he neared, Sally could only stare. He moved with the hard grace and quiet economy of effort unusual for a man so tall and muscularly built. Backlit by bright morning light, he was a sight too stimulating for a woman in her condition. When he placed an arm around her shoulders, the contact sent an involuntary thrill through her and she battled to squelch a gasp of surprise.

He leaned down. "I'm confident I can convince my

little sugarplum to add a hyphenated 'Step' to her name, Grandmother Vanderkellen.'' With his free hand he placed a finger under her chin and pressed upward. With his touch, Sally realized her mouth had opened in astonishment.

His fingertip prodded her lips together. An instant later his mouth covered hers. The kiss was brief, warm and gentle, the way a man might kiss his wife in the presence of family. But that's not how it felt. The heady sensation that surged through Sally was far from brief or gentle. But warm? Yes, Noah's kiss had been warm. Too warm. Her body sang with it, rang with it. Nerve endings zapped, snapped and sizzled, short-circuiting significant functions, like breathing, vision, speech and hearing.

When she became aware of her surroundings again, Noah was clear across the kitchen pouring coffee and grinning at Abigail. Apparently they'd gone on with their casual conversation, never noticing that she'd left the planet. She swallowed, grateful to discover she'd regained at least partial mobility and she could see and hear. She sucked in a long breath then blew it out.

A man's kiss had never caused her so much emotional turmoil before. Darn her raging hormones! Her wild reaction to a brief touch of his lips had to be due to that. Shaky and weak, she looked down at her bowl of oatmeal with raisins. Steam no longer rose from it. She made a puzzled face. Just how long had she been spaced-out? As Noah returned to the table with two mugs, she cast him a hard look.

"Here you go, darling." He set the piping hot brew

beside her right hand. "Abigail?" He handed the older woman her coffee.

"Thank you, Noah."

Sally glanced at her grandmother, wondering at the vague lilt in her voice. Was she actually starting to warm to him? Sally assumed the fact that Noah was a Texas hick, in Abigail's eyes, would outweigh even the fact that he was a doctor. If she truly found him appealing, then Noah had achieved a real coup, a displacement in prejudicial thinking of global proportion.

Worriedly chewing the inside of her cheek, she watched them chat. An ironic thought struck. How horrified would Abigail be if she knew the man she'd shouted cranky orders at for the last forty-eight hours, and whom she expected to wait on her hand-and-foot was, in actuality, a high-and-mighty Boston Barrett?

Sally's twenty-eighth birthday dawned on the fourth interminable day after the Vanderkellens first darkened her door. She'd stopped working during the early hours since it was so disruptive for her houseful of guests. But that made the possibility of having Vivica's cradle ready for her birth look more and more remote. Yet another of the many negatives to this unsettling situation.

As she blinked to a state of full wakefulness, she turned toward Noah, an unintentional deed that was done before her conscious mind could stop it. She was startled to discover he was gone. Sniffing the air, she thought she smelled coffee. She inhaled deeply of the rich aroma. Smiling, she stretched like a lazy cat. There was one thing about Noah she couldn't fault, and that was his coffee. If he was half the doctor he was coffeemaker he must be on a medical par with Jonas Salk or Dr. Spock. The biggest problem with having Noah Barrett as a woman's gynecologist and obstetrician was embarrassingly obvious. He was too gorgeous.

Sally lumbered up to sit, visualizing Noah in his doctor mode, his healer persona in place, as his hands...

A furious blush heated her cheeks. "Wow!" she mumbled. "That fantasy didn't take long to get racy!" Brushing hair out of her eyes, she slid her feet from beneath the covers. "Time to get up, get dressed, and most important," she ground out, *"get your mind off Noah's hands!"*

When she entered the kitchen, she wasn't surprised to see her fake husband sitting at the table, conversing with Abigail.

"Noah," the older woman said. "Be a good boy and bring me another cup of coffee."

He glanced up to see Sally at the door, his expression changing slightly. He'd been grinning, but when he saw her his smile widened a notch. "Of course, Grandmother." He stood, but before he headed toward the coffeepot, he walked to Sally's chair and pulled it out. "Good morning, sleepyhead."

Vivica kicked and Sally wondered if there was something about her own reaction to Noah's smile that telegraphed itself all the way to her unborn daughter. It seemed as if every time he aimed his smile her way, fake or not, Vivica reacted. Did the man's smile have such power he could even excite females yet to be born?

Tossing off the silly notion, probably brought on by sleep deprivation, Sally took up her playacting. "Thank you, sweetheart." She walked to the chair and presented her cheek to him for a husbandly peck. That was safer than chancing another lip-lock, even as brief as the one two days ago. Its effects had been hard on her, especially after the hot kiss that first night. She didn't want to feel so confused and flustered and stimulated. It kept her awake nights, made her lose her appetite. That couldn't be good for Vivica.

He accepted the prim invitation and kissed her, precariously near her lips. She wondered if the fact that he'd brushed the corner of her mouth with his lips had been his way of mocking her, or had it merely been an inattentive accident.

"Sit, darling. I'll serve."

She couldn't look at him right then and gathered herself by taking her napkin and placing it over her lap. She slid a glance at her grandmother's plate. It contained something that looked like a rolled up pancake stuffed with fruit and cottage cheese, topped with syrup. Whatever it was, it was definitely not the straight-from-the-store-container diet Abigail had subsisted on since her arrival. Three cheers for Noah the miracle worker.

"No yogurt this morning, Grandmother?"

Abigail took a bite of her rolled pancake dish, chewed and swallowed before she spoke. "When Noah offered to make strawberry and ricotta crepes, how could I refuse?"

Sally eyed the food. "That's a good question," she murmured as Noah handed her a plate. She also had no idea where crepes might have come from. "What's this?" she asked.

"Your breakfast."

She was startled. "Did you make this?"

His hand cupped her cheek with what felt like true affection. "Naturally. It's Sunday. I always make your favorite crepes on Sunday."

Sally had never had a crepe in her life. But since it looked like nothing more frightening than a skinny pancake, a little cheese, strawberries and maple syrup, she didn't figure it could be too terrible. "Oh—is it Sunday already?" she improvised. "Time does fly." In her estimation, time had crawled by like a sick snake, but she forced a smile. "It looks wonderful—as usual."

He seated himself. "Thank you."

"I would never have thought you Texas people would know anything about crepes." Abigail genteelly patted her lips with her napkin. "These are actually quite good."

Sally fought the urge to growl. Texas people? She'd said it with a grimace, as though the words left a bad taste in her mouth.

"We prefer cornmeal mush and sorghum." Noah winked in Sally's direction. "But crepes are good, too."

Abigail's gaze, trained on forking up another bite, went wide with dismay. Evidently the idea of eating something called mush was far down on her list of Things To Eat While In Texas. Sally had a hard time stifling a grin. Darn Noah and his teasing. Why couldn't he be serious? But even as she gave him a cautioning look, a little voice inside her was hailing his cheeky ribbing.

"It's Sally's favorite," he went on, seemingly only emboldened by her cautioning glare. "Isn't it, darling?"

She cleared her throat. That dratted, disobedient giggle was still trying to surface. What was her problem?

This was *not* funny! "Actually I love fried mush." She lifted her chin to indicate his teasing had not flustered her in the least. She did love fried mush. "But, being pregnant, I've cut down on fried foods."

"She's going to be a wonderful mother," Noah said, looking absolutely sincere, a masterly feat, since Sally knew how untruthful that statement was. He didn't think she knew what she was doing. Her annoyance billowed and she broke eye contact. Needing to do something, she took a bite of her crepe. "Oh—it's good," she said, then bit her tongue when she realized she'd spoken aloud. *You shouldn't be surprised, dummy! Sunday morning crepes are supposed to be a weekly thing!*

"She's always so sweet to compliment me, Grandmother," Noah said. "Thank you, love."

Sally refused to meet his gaze. For the charade, she compromised, glancing in his direction but aiming over his shoulder. She smiled and tried to look lovesick. "You're welcome—*darling.*"

She continued to eat, focusing desperately on her plate.

After a moment's tense silence, Abigail said, "Noah, why do you choose to practice medicine in this—this backwater wasteland? You should bring your wife to Boston. Unfortunately your rustic accent might hold you back for a while, but with the Vanderkellen contacts, you could go far. Be anything you care to be." She sighed audibly, a woman thoroughly put-upon. "I've tried and tried to convince Sam to move, but he is balking." A pause. "I believe he feels Sally *needs* him."

There was another pause, during which Sally had to clamp her jaws to keep from shouting *Sam can go wher-*

ever he pleases. I am not the idiot child who needs a keeper, simply because I take after my father more than my mother!

Noah cleared his throat. "I think it's time for my surprise."

Sally glanced at him, puzzled. What? More surprises? Wasn't the fact that he'd conjured up crepes enough for one breakfast? Could she cope with something else?

He disappeared in the direction of the entryway. Abigail viewed his exit with interest. "I wonder what he's doing?"

Sally swallowed her bite, not knowing what to say. Stalling she took a sip of coffee. After that, with Abigail staring at her, she decided she'd better respond with something. She smiled weakly. "Uh—Noah is full of surprises." That was lame, but she prayed her remark was vague enough, in case she was supposed to be in on this surprise.

She desperately hoped Noah would reenter with a fully recovered Hubert. She knew Noah had examined her grandfather several times. Perhaps this morning he was greatly improved and had confided in Noah that he wanted to surprise Abigail with the good news.

Her hope soared. Could it be possible? *Please, please let it be true!* What a wonderful birthday present that would be—to watch Abigail and Hubert disappear.

CHAPTER SEVEN

"YOU love him very much, don't you?"

Sally was still watching the empty door through which Noah had disappeared when her grandmother asked the question. Startled by such a personal observation from this woman who was hardly more than a stranger, she turned. "What?"

Abigail didn't smile, but she didn't get all puckery, either. She merely looked at her granddaughter. "I said, you love him very much. I can see it in your face."

Sally was astonished by such a crazy statement, but she couldn't tell her grandmother. Interestingly her cheeks helped the charade by going hot.

Abigail frowned, the expression more one of consideration than annoyance. "Don't be embarrassed, girl. He's a fine man."

Sally could only stare. She wanted to shout, *So was my father! You would have loved him if you'd given him half a chance! Instead, just because he wasn't up to your stuffy standards, you shunned your own daughter. You're a snooty, foolish woman and I don't care what you think!*

Sally felt a hand on hers. Cold fingers squeezed her own. "I'm glad you're naming your baby Vivica." Abigail's eyes glistened and it struck Sally that her grandmother's eyes were a soft, moss-green—like her own mother's had been. Abigail had spent so much of their time together squinty and distant, it was difficult for Sally to think of her as anyone but a stranger named Mrs. Vanderkellen, let alone as her mother's own mother.

Right now, shimmering as they were, those old eyes looked less severe, diminishing the cool, aloof bearing Sally was accustomed to seeing. For a flash she could see her mother in Abigail's face, and she experienced a twinge of sadness, yearning for a close family once again. There was her older brother Sam, yes, but he had his own life. Sally was basically alone, except for little Vivica…

The baby kicked. Sally removed her hand from Abigail's grip to lay it protectively over her restless baby. Abigail followed the movement, blinking several times. *Good heavens,* was she about to cry? Sally couldn't fathom where this familial sentiment was coming from after a self-imposed estrangement from their only daughter and grandchildren that spanned more than thirty years.

Maybe the fact that her baby's father was a doctor—at least Abigail *thought* Noah was the father—somewhat redeemed Sally the Welder for containing any genetic makeup from a working class Texan. A new surge of fury banished her fleeting softening toward the elderly woman with her mother's eyes.

Picking up her fork, she took another bite of crepe. When she finished, she murmured, "I loved my mother." Eyeing Abigail with as much civility as she could manage, she added, "Why shouldn't I name my baby in her honor? Your daughter was a wonderful person. I would never have given up one minute of our time together for *anything*."

Abigail seemed to wince, her pinched expression returning. It looked almost as though she'd been slapped. Sally felt a momentary pinprick of conscience for being spiteful, but she couldn't help it. She'd been stewing for too long and recently had had too little sleep.

"Well, well, I can see my surprises don't inspire much anticipation."

Sally jumped at the sound of Noah's voice. She shifted to watch him reenter the kitchen. He smiled at her. The sight blasted to bits all her bitterness and anger. Why that could happen, she didn't know, but her heart rate told her it was true. The *boom, boom, boom* in her chest was wreaking havoc on her ribs. If she weren't careful her surging pregnancy hormones would kill her yet.

Noah walked to her and knelt. Suddenly his face was nearly on a level with hers, though she still had to look slightly upward. "Happy birthday, sweetheart." His eyes seemed to look at her with true devotion. She had to give him credit for his acting. If she didn't know better, she'd swear he meant it.

His pronounced cheekbones and long, shiny black lashes were a striking sight, with morning sunshine pouring across him. Her raging hormones raged on. She wondered if he and Abigail could hear the thunderous pounding in her chest? The sound was deafening inside her head.

She stared, puzzled and wary. What was he up to? How did he know it was her birthday? She couldn't ask any questions in Abigail's presence, so she waited, hoping if he spoke she could read his lips, since she was afraid she wouldn't hear a thing over the hammering of her heart.

He lifted a small box, wrapped in metallic silver paper and a fancy red bow. "I hope you like it."

This whole scene was surreal. Noah knew it was her birthday and he had a gift for her? He hadn't even been gone from the place, except that first day when he'd mailed Sam's goggles and fetched persnickety Abigail's uncontaminated groceries. He'd hardly even known her name then, let alone that her birthday was in a few days.

She took the package, staring at it. "It—it's a lovely—box." She wondered what grocery store he'd been to where they did gift-wrapping. "What is it?"

"Why don't you open it and see?"

That was an idea. Funny, her brain was caught on some kind of snag. She seemed to be experiencing a strange case of fantasy-reality space warp. She was truly touched and surprisingly excited about Noah's gift.

Noah's gift.

Those two words summoned up a warm glow, and she wrapped herself in it. Another part of her kept harping in a strident voice that this was all a parlor trick, a prop. Some trinket he'd picked up at the grocery store. Probably a coupon for pitted prunes. *But Noah is giving you a gift,* another part of her reminded her through a sigh. The mental sigh startled her. She hoped the only outward sign was a couple of quick blinks.

Besides, since he was being bold enough to hand it to her in front of Abigail, it couldn't be a grocery store coupon. Could it? She toyed with the ribbon, then met his gaze. "Should—should I open it, now?" She tried desperately to telegraph her dilemma. If it was an empty box and she opened it in front of Abigail, the jig would be up. "Here?"

"Of course." He glanced briefly at Abigail. "Grandmother won't mind being a part of our celebration. Will you, Grandmother?" His attention returned to focus fully on Sally. The pseudoadoration in his gaze brought real tears to her eyes. So much so that she had to blink them back. Maybe she was a better actor than she gave herself credit for, too. With a nod and a lump in her throat, she began to remove the wrappings.

Her fingers actually shook.

She lay aside the wrapping and lifted the lid of the small white box. Inside was a black velvet jewelry case. She gasped. Apparently that first day he'd been somewhere besides the grocery store and the post office. She'd never seen vegetables or stamps sold in velvet cases. "Oh—I can't imagine..."

Lifting the elegant black box, she gazed at it then transferred her attention to Noah. She tried to say something but didn't know what—at least not in front of Abigail. With a difficult swallow, she opened it. Inside lay a lovely golden bracelet, dotted all the way around with dainty diamondlike stones. They couldn't be real, of course. But they looked genuine. She bit her trembling lower lip and lifted the delicate gift. It sparkled in the sunlight. "Oh—oh, Noah, it's so...perfect."

"Perfection for perfection, darling," he said softly. When he lifted the bracelet from her fingers, her gaze flashed back to his face. "Let's see it on."

She lay its case in her lap, reflexively withdrawing her hands. "Oh—it's too pretty." She glanced at her callused palm, her blunt nails, the small burns that went with her work. She never wore rings or bracelets, not wanting to draw attention to her work-roughened hands. They were far from her best feature. "It's too pretty…" Clenching her hand, she dropped it into her lap and gave him an apologetic look.

His brows had dipped, though his smile remained intact, as if he were incredulous at her refusal. With a shake of his head, he grasped her fisted hand, lifted it, warm fingers uncurling hers. "You have beautiful hands. Artist's hands." He lowered his face to her palm and kissed it, murmuring, "Never be ashamed." His gaze met hers again and he winked, the tiny act so clearly a silent assertion of approval, she was stunned by the impact. Before she could recover, Noah had fastened the bracelet to her wrist.

She watched, but felt oddly detached from reality. Her palm, where he kissed her and murmured compliments against her skin, was all she could feel. His eyes, when he'd looked at her, cautioning her gently never to be ashamed of her hands, was all she could see.

Though he smiled and spoke to her, whatever he said became mere bits of fluff floating on the edges of her conscience. He had let her go, so she stared down at her hand, with the bracelet encircling her wrist. Turning her arm she looked at the work-hardened palm. Stared at the calluses. *Try to get yourself under control, Sally,* her logical side shouted. *He's acting. Of course, he didn't really mean—*

She felt a male hand slide along her jaw to cup her nape. A heated wave of breath caressed her mouth. An instant later gentle, persuasive lips met hers, sending fire through her veins. She trembled as his fingers spread over the back of her head, the pressure of his hand a tender invitation to deepen the kiss. She was conscious only of his intimate nearness, his scent. Her senses throbbed with it, triggering primitive yearnings.

What he could do with such an innocent touch of his lips was hot and wild, and she wrapped her arms around him, sighing against his mouth.

She heard a low, feral growl and suddenly the kiss was over. Dazed she could only stare, trying to focus. Noah had backed away, though his hand still rested on her shoulder. "Goodness, woman," he said. "In front of your grandmother, too." There was a pause. Sally watched him, blurry though he was. She sensed he'd turned toward Abigail. "You'll have to forgive my wife," he said, his tone husky. "She's forever trying to seduce me. I fear for my reputation."

Abigail cleared her throat. "Well—the bracelet is a lovely gift."

Sally took in a breath, trying to see straight. Noah finally slid his hand from around her neck.

"Thank you, Grandmother," he said. "It came from right here in Texas. Imagine that."

Noah's tone definitely held a teasing note. When Sally could see again, she cast a worried glance at Abigail. The woman's brow was wrinkled, nothing new. "There's no need to be facetious, Noah," she admonished. "My remarks about Texas have merely been an attempt to encourage you to enhance your position."

The bracelet felt strange on her wrist, and Sally looked down at it. Even in the shadow of the table, it sparkled. Somehow the gift gave her courage and she looked

Abigail straight in the eye. "Neither of us needs to enhance our position."

"Texas is a wonderful place to live and raise a family," Noah said with a smile. "My facetiousness was merely an attempt to encourage you to enhance your opinion."

Shrewd green eyes met gorgeous blue. Sally watched as Abigail's expression eased, if only slightly. "Touché, son." She turned away and picked up her coffee. "Happy birthday, Sally," she murmured gravely. As Abigail sipped, her glance remained fixed on thin air somewhere above the rim of her mug.

After breakfast Sally carefully laid the bracelet on her dresser, since she worked in her studio most of the day. It wouldn't do to allow such a lovely piece of jewelry to be damaged. All day long, as she worked on her commissioned metal art, her mind skipped and skittered to that morning, Noah's gift and his oh-so-sweet-and-steamy birthday kiss.

During dinner, Sally found herself less emotionally tied up in knots over her unwanted imprisonment with Abigail and Hubert. She'd even found herself smiling at a story Noah related to Abigail about a set of twins he'd delivered, at a bus stop outside a restaurant where he'd been eating lunch.

All in all, today had been a surprisingly nice birthday. Except for the periodic false labor pains and her aching back. Tired, but in a strangely buoyant mood even though her back was giving her fits, Sally entered her bedroom. Fresh from a shower, she wore her favorite fleecy robe and fuzzy slippers. Noah wasn't there, but she knew he checked on Hubert every evening, so she wasn't surprised.

A twinkle on her dresser caught her eye and she found herself smiling. The bracelet seemed to cheerfully beckon. She didn't hesitate to answer its call. Perching on the dresser's chair, she lifted the jewelry from the open velvet box and lay it across her wrist. A delicate, lovely thing, exactly what she would have chosen if she'd had her choice of a million bracelets.

Without thinking about it, she closed the clasp and held up her arm so the overhead light would catch the stones and make them flicker.

The door clicked and Sally knew Noah had returned. "Hi," she said, twisting around to greet him with a smile. Dropping her arm, she folded her hands in her lap. "How is Grandfather?"

Noah's grin was crooked. "He still won't try to get up. Insists he would instantly die in agony." He shook his head. "I'm beginning to believe your grandmother was right. The guy has no intention of visiting any pyramids."

Sally laughed, once again surprised by her light-hearted mood. "He acts like a spoiled little boy. And Abigail is his stern but ineffectual nanny."

Noah walked to the bed, his boot-heels rapping against the pine floor. He sat on the side nearest the dresser. Leaning forward, he rested his forearms on his thighs. His grin remained intact.

He wore jeans and a soft, knit shirt the same blue as his eyes. He made quite a picture and Sally let herself take him in. "Ineffectual but incessant," he said with the rakish lift of an eyebrow. "The woman harps at him constantly. He's either the most obstinate man I've ever seen or the most harassed. If I were him, I'd be out of that bed by now, if only to shut her up.''

Sally laughed, astonished at herself for feeling so cheerful. "I would never guess you were annoyed with her, considering the gallant way you treat her. She thinks you're darling.''

"Sure, she does.'' Noah was clearly skeptical. "I've never seen so much grimacing and pouting from one face in my life.'' He shrugged broad shoulders. "I can usually get women to warm to me fairly easily.''

I'll just bet you can! Sally threw out mentally. "She's absolutely warm for you.'' Sally turned in her seat to better face him. "I don't know her well, but my guess is, for her to suggest you move us to Boston, well, that's got to be on a par with the Queen of England knighting somebody.''

"You forget, she hates my rustic accent.''

He winked and the sexy playfulness of the act made her heart perform an appreciative leap. "If she only knew. If you chose to, you could out-Boston-speak even her.''

He straightened and peered at the ceiling. "Yeah, well…''

Sally experienced a prick of foreboding. "What?''

He shook his head. "Nothing, I'm just…''

He let the sentence drop. She bit her lip, fearing she could read his thoughts. "Wanting to get on with your vacation, I know.''

Their eyes met and she experienced an overwhelming need to show how much she appreciated the sacrifice he was making. Reaching out, she touched his knee. A big, solid, masculine knee. She was shocked by how special the contact seemed, since the body part was nothing more intimate than a denim-swathed chunk of bone and sinew.

She experienced a surge of naughty guilt, but squashed it down. How silly! She owed Noah Barrett a great debt of gratitude, and an appreciative touch was essential. She would have preferred a hug. But considering the unsettling fact that she couldn't get his kisses out of her head, a hug was much too dangerous. "I don't know how I'll ever repay you for what you're doing," she murmured. "Any suggestions?" *Good grief, Sally!* She silently scolded. *If that question didn't have sexual overtones I don't know what would!*

His glance dipped to where her hand lay on his knee, then returned to her face. "You put on the bracelet."

She scanned the jewelry. "Yes." Looking at her fingers spread over his knee, she remembered with affection how he'd kissed her roughened palm and murmured she had artist hands. All day long that kiss, that soft compliment, stayed with her. Suddenly her worst feature, the hands her ex-fiancé had insisted where not the hands of a doctor's wife, had become artist's hands. She lifted her gaze to Noah's face, his eyes. Her smile refreshed itself. With that one, quiet assurance he'd done wonders for her self-esteem. "How did you know it was my birthday?"

He leaned back, resting his palms on the bed. "Yesterday, while you were in your studio, Sam called to let me know the goggles got there. He told me about your birthday."

"Oh?" She wanted to ask about Noah's girlfriend.

How he felt about not being with her, but she didn't want to hear his answer. "So—uh…" Struggling to get her mind off his ladylove, she said the next thing that came to her. "So—when did you have time to shop?"

He appeared confused. "Shop?"

She held up the bracelet. "For my birthday?"

As she turned her wrist to show off the sparkle, he watched, his brow wrinkled. After a few seconds, he seemed to comprehend what she meant, his confused expression taking on a troubled air. "Oh, the bracelet." His gaze met hers, his features solemn. "The gift was part of the illusion." He leaned forward again, rested his forearms on his thighs and clasped his hands. "I had it with me, so…" He paused. His jaw muscles bunched, indicating agitation. His eyes took on what Sally feared might be a glimmer of pity. "I thought you understood."

I thought you understood.

That one sentence, spoken softly, blue eyes full of pity, took only a flash for Sally to digest.

I thought you understood.

The truth hit like a blast of icy water. He hadn't bought the bracelet for her at all. *He'd bought it for his girlfriend!* When Sam mentioned Sally's birthday, Noah decided to play the lie to the hilt, pretending to give her another woman's gift.

Pretending.

Of course. And why not? Their whole relationship was based on fiction. How could she have thought he was really giving *her* that beautiful gift?

She swallowed hard, striving to drag her heart out of the dark pit it had tumbled into. *How stupid can you be, Sally?* An even harder question to answer was, *Why does the truth hurt so much?* Could she actually be such an idiot?

"Understood?" she echoed, fighting hard for a smile that would suggest she had understood all along. "Of course, I do—*I did.*" With fierce determination to appear nonchalant, she lifted the bracelet once more and turned it in the light. No wonder the stones looked so much like diamonds. For his real girlfriend, he would buy *real* diamonds.

This time, she avoided looking at her hand. Lord, the kiss on her palm. All part of the illusion. Closing her hand, she dropped it into her lap. "I—was just—trying it on for—laughs." She grinned. It hurt her cheeks, but with a quick peek in the mirror she was gratified to see it looked real. "I meant, how did my birthday come up—on the phone?" That was weak, but it was the best she could do and keep from bursting into stupid tears.

She met his eyes, resolved to be adult about this. So something in her brain had short-circuited, making her forget the fraud for a little while. So what? She knew she had rough hands and—and besides, she didn't even wear bracelets!

"He told me to give you a birthday kiss for him."

"Oh—I see." The fact that Noah's kiss hadn't been his idea, either, was too depressing to allow fully into her mind. "Well..." She fumbled with the clasp. "It was a great—gag. Thanks for thinking of it. It was very—realistic."

Slipping the bracelet off she replaced it in the box, snapped it closed and handed it to him. "If you ask my opinion? We did good." She held desperately to her smile. Her heart aching for a reprieve from those sympathetic eyes, she hoisted herself off the chair. "Now, if you'll excuse me. I'm pooped."

It was all she could do to get into bed and barricade herself behind her fortress of pillows before silly tears escaped to tremble on her lashes. Stuffing a pillow against her mouth, she strangled an absurd need to blubber.

Sally knew her pregnancy's exploding hormone levels could affect her emotions, but she had no idea they could make her so dumb.

Noah remained hunched on the edge of Sally's bed, staring down at the velvet box. Jane's bracelet. He fingered the case, his thoughts turning back to yesterday's telephone conversation with Sam. The discussion about the goggles and Sally's birthday weren't the only topics explored.

Jane, it seemed, had met an old college gal pal—*and* her older brother, doctor something-or-other, a plastic surgeon. It seemed the doctor had taken it upon himself to relieve Jane's loneliness. According to Sam's cynical report, Jane was completely agreeable to being—relieved.

Noah found himself crushing the box, not in a fit of jealous rage but with an indignant stab of injured ego. Why wasn't he furious that his almost-fiancée, his one and only female companion for two years, so quickly and readily flounced into another man's arms?

It could all be innocent. Their evenings out could be threesomes, with Jane's school friend along to chaperon. In his gut, he suspected otherwise. And Sam had said the "duo," which meant two, not three, had been "practically inseparable.'' Sam's tone had inferred day *and* night. Naturally Sam couldn't be absolutely sure...

He shook his head. Funny, he was more aggravated than covetous, and that surprised him. He unclenched his fist from around the box and opened it, staring unemotionally at the gold and diamonds.

Somehow the bracelet didn't seem right for Jane any longer. It wasn't even because she might be having a sexual fling behind his back. The jewelry just didn't *feel* right for Jane, now. Not because he felt betrayed, because he didn't, which was nuts. Even more nuts than that, he could almost see her side. Having her boyfriend be a no-show on what was supposed to have been two weeks of hot and sexy tropical nights. He might have done the same thing in her position.

Snapping the box closed, he clenched his teeth, the realization unsettling him. What did that say about their relationship? If he was willing to forgo a week with her—promised to her—to do a bizarre favor for a virtual stranger?

If it was true that Jane felt no qualms about jumping into the sack with the first acceptable male, what did that say about their connection? What exactly was their relationship? What were they to each other? Lovers? Friends? Mere convenience? He supposed he'd never analyzed it. There hadn't been any need. They'd both been satisfied with the status quo. His work kept him so busy, he and Jane hadn't had time to do more than eat out and sleep...

He cringed. They hadn't talked, gotten to know each other, deepened their relationship. If that was even what either of them had wanted. He dragged a hand through his hair. What did he want from Jane? What did she want from him? It was something he'd better think about. He eyed the velvet box in his hand. Yes. It was something he needed to think about very seriously.

A muffled sound caught his attention and he stilled, listening.

It came again, louder. A moan? He shifted to view the blockade of pillows across the bed from him. "Sally, are you okay?"

"It's—just false—" she abruptly bit off her sentence and groaned "—labor."

She sounded strained, in pain. Dropping the jewel box, he jumped up and rounded the bed. "How often have the pains been coming?"

She wiped at her eyes with fisted knuckles. "Just a few pains every couple of hours." She winced as another contraction took her breath.

"Let me help."

She opened one eye. "Thanks, but they already hurt enough."

"Very funny." He took her hand. "Come with me." Gently he tugged, encouraging her to sit.

She didn't.

"Come where?" she wheezed, resistant and clearly suspicious.

He wasn't taking no for an answer. Throwing back the covers, he lifted her from her pillow fort. "We're going to take a bath."

CHAPTER EIGHT

SALLY couldn't believe it. One minute she was buried in her pillow fort, feeling sorry for herself and trying to ignore the iron vise squeezing her midsection. The next she was being whisked away in Noah's arms. And was she crazy, or had he said both *we* and *bath,* in the same sentence?

"What do you mean *we're* going to take a bath?" she demanded, through pain-clenched teeth. "I just took a shower!"

"This is to ease your pain."

She wriggled in revolt. "I can do that by walking around."

"Trust me. This will be better."

"Oh, yeah? For you or me?" She pressed her hands against his chest to protest his macho-man behavior. "If you think I'm going to take a bath with you, you've lost—"

"I'm not getting in the tub."

He carried her into the hallway. "You bet your boots you're not," she said in her sternest whisper. She didn't want the Vanderkellens to hear. The strong contraction crushing her belly made her cringe. The next thing she knew she was in the bathroom being settled in the old clawfoot tub.

"Take your gown off and start the tap. Run it luke-warm." He turned toward the linen shelf. Drawing out a large white bath sheet, he laid it over the side of the tub. "Once you're undressed, spread this across the bathtub for modesty. If you feel the need."

She glared at him from her seat on the chilly porcelain. *"If?"* she echoed, making sure he read the statement, *You are a raving lunatic!* in her expression.

His lips seemed to twitch with humor, but only for a second, so she couldn't be positive. "Sally," he said, sounding perfectly sane and serious. "I *am* a doctor. Naked women are my business."

She clamped her hands on the curved rim of the tub. "Well, you're not *my* doctor, and my naked body is *not* your busin—" She abruptly cut off her sentence, hunching in pain as another contraction clasped her abdomen in its harsh grasp.

"I promise, this will help," he said. "I'll be back in five minutes for your back massage."

She heard the door click shut. After a few seconds, she looked up to stare after him. "You have some nerve, Dr. Barrett!" she muttered, but she only hesitated for another half minute before starting to unbutton her granny gown. Her aching back could use a massage. *And he is a doctor,* a little voice in her brain urged. *I'm sure he's completely unfazed by the sight of a naked, pregnant woman.*

She swallowed, amazed as she watched herself separating the front of her gown. What was wrong with her fingers? Why were they going along with this "massage your back" madness? As she struggled to determine why her hands were committing mutiny, she began to wriggle around to work the gown up over her hips so her similarly mutinous arms could fling it off.

By the five-minute deadline, tap water half-filled the tub with mildly warm water. The bath sheet was spread across the tub and Sally clutched the nearest terry edge beneath her chin. There was precious little she could do about hiding her back. Luckily the overhead bulb was only a forty-watter. Maybe with the water and dimness, her backside would be too wavy and dusky for him to see.

When his knock came, it boomed like a cannon in her head, and she jumped. She knew her reaction was due to nerves. He'd actually tapped very lightly, since he, too, was aware the Vanderkellens were right across the hall.

She cleared her throat. "Come in." Evidently even her capacity to speak had joined the rebellion. She'd planned to say, "I changed my mind. I don't want any massage. *Go away!*" Why hadn't that been what her insubordinate lips uttered? The door clicked open and shut. Mortified heat swept up her cheeks as the rap of his boot-heels on tile signaled his approach.

Unable to look at him, she swept her gaze across the pedestal sink to the moss-colored tiles that covered the bathroom floor and walls to waist level. Lifting her gaze further, she focused on the floral wallpaper of snowy dogwood blossoms, and tried to concentrate on how it brightened the room.

Dogwoods were her mother's favorite spring bloom. After she died, Sally had kept her mind and hands occupied by repapering the bath with the cheerful design. Nervous to the point of light-headedness, she made herself scrutinize the dainty flowers with the touch of pink on each delicate petal. Her own two dogwood trees—

planted years ago by her dad, a birthday gift to her mother—would be spectacular in another week or two.

"How do you feel?"

His question made her gasp. She jerked so badly she nearly pulled the bath sheet into the water. Clearing her throat, she carefully smoothed the terry across the tub. "I—I'm not totally comfortable with this."

"Not totally comfortable?" He chuckled. "That's the mother of all understatements."

He was behind her and she cringed. "What are you looking at?" She knew a little about scuba diving since she'd taken the course with Sam. One fact she recalled way too vividly, how water magnified things by twenty-five percent. Did her backside look twenty-five percent bigger?

A hand on her nape made her lurch with alarm.

"Calm down, Sally," Noah said. "I'm putting up your hair." She felt him twist the stuff into a knot. "As for what I'm looking at…" He paused to place the clip securely. The delay was so badly timed, she wanted to scream. "I'm looking at your back," he finally finished.

Flinching, she closed her eyes. "Try not to."

He didn't speak, but his hands moved from the knotted hair to her shoulders where his fingers began a gentle massage. "You're very tense."

"How silly of me," she shot back. "Strange men spend scads of time in my bathroom feeling me up!"

"Take it easy. I'm a doctor. I don't feel women up."

"So you *call* it an examination—or—or a massage. A rose by any other name is still feeling me up!"

"Hush. Take some deep breaths," he said. "This won't work if you don't try to relax."

Easy for him to say! "Do you massage many of your patients?" she asked, trying not to think about how heavenly his fingers felt against her skin.

"No. Breathe."

She opened her eyes and frowned, but didn't dare look back at him. She sucked in a shuddery breath and blew it out. From her peripheral vision she could see a knee to her left. She peeked right. Another knee. Good Lord, he was straddling her, sitting on the tub's rounded edge. She felt very, very intimately surrounded by the man. "You *don't* massage your patients?" she croaked. She couldn't believe that. He was much too good. "So, you say you're making this up as you go along?"

"You're still tense," he said. "Try to relax." His hands dipped lower, working to ease tension along her spine. She had never been massaged before. But she had an innate sense this was a very good example of what a massage should be. She wanted to sigh long and loud, but she forced herself to keep such tattletale displays locked inside. He didn't need to know she was melting, her feminine side unduly stimulated. After all, she was about as close to a man's erotic ideal as a beached whale.

"That's better," he said. "Take slow, deep breaths, and I'll answer your question."

She nodded and sucked in another big draught.

His fingers smoothed taut skin. The pressure easing the ache in her back. He worked without speaking. The silence stretched on.

"I'm *breathing*," she said through an inhale. If she kept up this pace, she'd pass out from hyperventilation. "Answer my question."

"Breathe *slowly*. You're not running a marathon."

What did he know? Her heart was pounding like a marathon runner's. Deliberately she slowed her breaths. "Are you going to answer me or are you just going to criticize my respiratory system?"

"Okay." His fingers kneaded and pleasured. "I learned massage from a college roommate. I don't personally massage my patients, but I have shown a number of spouses how to ease Braxton-Hicks." His hands caressed. With firm, solid pressure, his fingers mastered her tenseness, eased her pain. The effect bordered on miraculous. "Try to think of false labor as your body practicing for childbirth."

She wished she could think of something, *anything,* besides his hands. They dipped lower, lower, relieving, yet stimulating her to the very bottom-most limits of propriety. Even so, all she could do was swallow hard and enjoy, revel, delight in his touch. She heard a sigh and realized with horror that she'd lost her precarious hold on her effort to hide her arousal. Quickly she masked it with a cough.

Angry with herself, she took it out on him. "All this pain is my body practicing, huh? Easy for you to say. Do you have any concept of the pain I'm feeling?"

He didn't speak for a moment. Then another, as his hands massaged, working their wizardry on her aching back. She felt good. Really good. By some mysterious sorcery on his part, her hostility drained away. Against her volition, she relaxed.

"Don't hold it against me for being a man," he said at last.

Oh, darling, a wayward little voice whispered, *I'd*

*give heaven and earth to be able to hold any little ol'
thing against you.*

She started. What kind of lewd thinking was that? She
was having very bold and startling thoughts about a doctor who was only doing her a favor. *Get your mind away
from lovemaking, Sally!* Overstimulated, she drew away
from his touch. "That's enough," she said. "I'm all
better now."

"Are you sure?"

"Just get your hands out of the water and *back off!*"

He didn't speak. Didn't move. After a tense minute,
his encompassing knees disappeared and she heard shuffling. "You're welcome. It was my pleasure."

She winced at his gibe, but kept her eyes averted and
her mouth shut.

"Let me help you out." His hand appeared before her
face.

She hated the fact that he was behaving gallantly after
her snippy behavior. Angry with herself, she eyed his
extended hand from beneath her lashes. She'd almost
completely quit taking baths, changing to showers, when
clambering out of a tub became too awkward and haz-
ardous. Though she hated the idea of accepting his help,
she knew it would be foolhardy to reject his offer.

Lifting her gaze to meet his solemn face, she shrugged
in apology. "I'm sorry I was rude. I just..." She didn't
know how to explain her behavior. *You got me so turned
on, my only choices were to snap at you or jump you,*
didn't seem like the best idea.

"I can't explain it," she said, opting for as much truth
as possible without actually telling the truth. "Please,
forgive me."

His brows dipped downward. "Do you think you're the first pregnant woman to snap at me? It's a hazard of my job."

A hazard of his job. That said it all. He'd turned her into such a quaking, aroused mess she'd barked at him like a junkyard dog, but to him the whole episode could be summed up as a *hazard* of the job.

He extended his fingers further, indicating that she take his hand. "Get out of there before you start to prune."

Reluctantly she accepted his offer. With her free hand, she grasped the bath sheet in a death grip. Seemingly without effort, he drew her up to stand. She was gratified that she managed to maintain her modesty throughout. He also helped her step from the tub, which was more dicey in the modesty department, since his warm hand came down low on her naked back to steady her as she stepped to the tile floor.

Overall, she made it without undue humiliation. The instant his hand released hers, she made quick work of wrapping her girth securely in the towel. Coercing herself to be brave, she faced him, attempting a grateful smile. "Thank you. I really do feel better."

He nodded, his expression stony. She noticed he'd backed away, and was leaning against the door, as though the place wasn't big enough for them both. Could she blame him for being in a hurry to leave? It was late, she was no prize to be around and he probably wanted to get to bed.

"It's too bad you don't have a husband," he said, sounding gruff. "He could—" For some reason, he didn't finish. She watched as his jaw muscles bunched.

She didn't like the direction of this conversation, even though it had been abruptly terminated. Apparently he'd decided against chastising her for what he thought of as her flawed decision to have a baby alone. It was too bad for him his decision to keep his views on the subject to himself had come a second too late.

"Look, Noah," she said, her ire flaring to life. "I know how you feel about what I've done. If I haven't said it before, I'm saying it now. Keep your opinions to yourself. I can do fine without a husband to massage my back or help raise my daughter!" She jutted her chin, not only irritated but oddly deflated. "From now on, I won't trouble you when my body goes into—*practicing!*" She managed to loosen a couple of fingers from their grasp on her towel, and indicated the door. *"Good night."*

His expression grim, he pursed his lips, as though working to keep from responding. With a brief nod of acquiescence, he turned away.

An instant later he was gone.

Sally's mood mutated from focused indignation to muddled gloom. She staggered to the wooden chair beside the sink and sat down. Suddenly weak and sick at heart, she buried her face in her hands, praying hard she wasn't falling in love with Noah Barrett. Praying hard that what she felt was entirely hormonal. All she needed now was to have her heart trampled by another my-way-or-the-highway *doctor*—even if his touch was paradise on earth.

Sally didn't know how it happened. Probably karma for lying to her grandparents about being married in the first place. After spending all day Monday avoiding Noah when possible, then forcing a loving smile when they had to be together in front of her grandmother, how had *he* ended up with her at her Prepared Childbirth class? Worse than that, how did she end up with *his* chest against *her* back, *her* body reclining between *his* legs? The one measly pillow supporting her lumbar area was paltry insulation from the heat his body radiated.

Talk about your basic nightmare!

Of all the men in the universe, why did he have to be the one holding her against him, his scent taunting, his hard, male body her sole support. She was mad at him, for Pete's sake! Mad at his "To choose single motherhood is deplorable!" attitude. She didn't want to be cuddled against him. Not merely because she was mad, either. He was too stimulating a pallet, and she was furious with herself for thinking like that.

"You're not relaxing your thigh, Sally," he murmured, his breath tormenting her ear.

She knew she wasn't relaxing her thigh. How did he expect her thigh to relax with his hand on it? "This really isn't necessary. I'm an expert at this, already. I don't need you giving me a pop quiz on relaxation."

"Your neuromuscular dissociation exercises are important," he said, his warm breath cruelly titillating. "This is a transfer skill you need. It teaches you how to relax other muscles during labor while your uterus is tense."

"I know what it's for!" she whispered tersely, trying not to draw attention to them. She peered around. The seven other couples were concentrating on each other as they practiced the relaxation exercise. Their teacher moved among them, smiling and chatting. She was several couples away. "I'm simply not in the mood tonight," she said under her breath.

His hand lay on her thigh, heating tense muscles. "Come on," he coaxed. She had a feeling her insubordination was trying even his well-ingrained bedside manner. "Relax that thigh. Prove to me you can."

She wanted to shout that he was being unfair. That the exercise was supposed to *start* with the pregnant partner completely free from unwanted stress. She was not free from unwanted stress. Noah's chest supporting her back, his inner thighs against her hips, were all unwanted stress. But how did she tell him that? How did she blurt out, *You're so sexy, you smell so good, I can't think of anything but turning over and planting a big, hot kiss on your lips and running my tongue...* She cleared her throat. This was bad, very bad. Going up in flames over a man was not like her and she was not happy with this new, inflamed Sally she was turning into. In heaven's name, she was eight months pregnant. She was supposed to be concentrating on creation, not procreation.

"My hormones are giving me trouble tonight," she muttered.

"What?" He leaned down, his lips so near her ear she could feel them brush the sensitive shell.

"I said," she swallowed to ease the rusty squeak in her voice. "My hormones are giving me trouble tonight. I'm—I'm antsy. I can't relax." That was true enough. "Maybe it's—my grandparents. They're stressing me out." There was truth in that statement, too.

He sat back, but she could feel his exhale against her

hair. "Look, the class is almost over. Relax one thigh for me and we can pack it in."

He drove a hard bargain. Deciding she had nothing to lose by trying, she took a deep breath and closed her eyes. Focusing on a blank screen in her head, she struggled to put his feel, his scent, the strong pull of his masculine sexuality from her mind. *Relax, you stupid thigh! No! Don't yell at it. Be quietly prompting as you breathe deep, slow, cleansing breaths. Relax little thigh. Relax even though his big, hot, sexy hand— No! Not good, relaxing thinking!*

She took another breath. *You can do this, Sally,* she counseled inwardly. *Pretend it's just Sam. Your big, lummox of a doctor-brother, Sam, who promises you a bowl of peach ice cream if you relax your muscles.*

She focused on her favorite, peach ice cream—on the texture, the taste, the sinful caloric overindulgence pregnancy allowed.

"That's better," he whispered. "I can feel you relaxing."

Her eyes popped wide. *Him!* For an instant she'd forgotten it was *him!*

"What happened? You're tense again."

She pushed herself up and away from his chest. "That's it for me. I'm done. I relaxed my thigh. Let's get out of here."

"Sally?" the instructor said. "Are you leaving?"

"Gladys…" She scrambled clumsily to stand. "Dr. Barrett has—to go," she improvised lamely. "But I'll practice at home. I promise."

Gladys was a tall, ripe-bodied redhead with a face full

of freckles. She passed Noah a concerned look. "Dr. Barrett, I hope it's nothing serious."

Sally peered at him, daring him to contradict her. He tossed off the pillow that had supported Sally's lower back, and stood. His expression was friendly, though Sally detected exasperation in his eyes. "I hope not, too." He held out a hand. "It was a pleasure to meet you, Gladys."

Though the instructor was a woman in her mid-forties, she blushed like a schoolgirl. "Oh, Dr. Barrett, it was wonderful of Sally to bring you." She shook his hand with gusto. "I've had a number of your patients in my classes, and they all praise you to the heavens."

When Gladys let go, she looked at Sally, her smile dimming slightly. "Dear, you look flushed. Are you okay?"

Sally feared that observation would not help ease her blush, but she nodded. "I'm fine. It was a little hot in here tonight. That's all."

"Oh?" Gladys, in her bulky sweater, seemed surprised. "Goodness, I—"

"Probably hormones," Sally cut in. She turned to Noah and took his hand, tugging. "We'd better go."

He glanced at her for a split second, then back at Gladys. "Yes, we'd better."

Gladys nodded and clapped her hands for attention. "Everybody, Sally and Dr. Barrett are going. Dr. Barrett, we want to thank you for your words of encouragement and support."

The class began to clap. Noah smiled and nodded as Sally pulled him toward the exit. Once outside in the hallway of the YMCA, he tugged her to a halt, challenging her with a dark look. "What's with you to-night?"

The only thing she could clearly think about was her hand clamped in his. To get her brain on track, she tugged free. She had no explanation that would do. Instead she fell back on the tradition she and Sam had established. "Could we go for a bowl of peach ice cream?" She indicated vaguely toward the exit. "There's a place not far away that serves the best in Houston."

His brows knit further. "You had to rush out of class because you crave peach ice cream?"

She shrugged. "If it'll get me a bowl, then yes, that's why I rushed us out. I'm craving it. *Bad!*"

He shook his head like a reprimanding schoolmaster. "Ice cream is not a good reason to sneak out of class early."

"I didn't sneak!" She knew that was beside the point, but it was the best she could do under the circumstances. "You stay if you want and relax your own muscles. Feel all smug and superior. I can walk to the ice-cream parlor perfectly well all by myself."

She stomped away.

"Whoa." He caught up, taking her arm. "What's all the hostility?"

"So typical! You think you know everything!" she shot back. "I am entirely capable of relaxing any dratted muscle in my body. When the time comes I'll do an impeccable job." He walked beside her as she berated him, past his truck, across an intersection, toward a brightly lit ice-cream parlor. "I'll do the most *impeccable* muscle-relaxing job ever. It's just that you make me nervous. You think by having this baby alone, I'm doing a dumb thing. You think single women can't competently raise a child alone. You find fault with every single thing I do. Why should any of *that* make me tense?''

He remained silent and continued to hold her arm as she sped along. Was he being a gentleman or only making sure she didn't break for freedom? Even if it was just to make sure she didn't escape, it was probably a good thing to do—supporting a hefty pregnant woman, in case she tripped over a crack in the pavement. There were a few cracks. For baby Vivica's sake she didn't jerk out of his hold. That didn't mean it wasn't at the top of her wish list. The erotic effect of his touch was disconcerting.

''Peach?'' He opened the parlor door and allowed her to precede him into a brightly lit room of pastel striped walls and noisy pop music.

A few other people sat at small, metal-legged tables with round, wood surfaces. Several teenage couples on dates talked and laughed, oblivious to the newest duo. One mother with a toddler in pink sat near the ice-cream counter. A foursome of gray-haired women in bowling shirts huddled beside the picture window, tittering like young girls.

''Pick a table,'' he said, not sounding particularly cheerful.

Without looking his way, she indicated the nearest one. ''This will do. Peach ice cream tastes good no matter where you eat it—or *who* you eat it with.'' She grabbed a chair and sat down before he could help her. She could tell he noticed her hurried plunge into a seat, by his hesitation. Without comment he seated himself in the chair beside hers. A waitress came over, her popping gum heralding her arrival.

"Hi, Sally," she said, scribbling on her pad. "Usual?"

"Uh-huh." She smiled at the gangly teenager with multicolored hair. As always, her yellow uniform was splotched with ice cream, her matching ball cap, with Gumbo's Best stitched in swirling navy across the brim was pulled low over purple bangs that nearly hid her eyes.

The waitress looked at Noah, apparently noticing for the first time he wasn't Sam. "Oh—hi, there." She stopped cracking her gum and gave him a lascivious once-over. "You're new."

Noah's grin was lopsided and humorless. "Not as new as you are."

The waitress had to think about that for a second, but when she got it, she laughed, glancing at Sally. "He yours?"

Sally couldn't believe the question and stared for a couple of beats before she got her wits back. "Just take his order, Myra."

She commenced chomping her gum and smirked slyly at Noah. "What'll ya have, cowboy? *Besides* my phone number?"

"Coffee."

She winked at him. "Comin' right up." When she walked away, Sally noticed a definite wiggle in the area of her skinny backside that she never recalled seeing before.

"Well, mercy me—*cowboy*." She placed her hands

together under her chin in a coy pose and flapped her lashes, mocking Myra's obvious come-on. "Is that the way you affect all waitresses?"

He leaned slightly toward her, resting a forearm on the table, eyes sparking with temper. "How can you doubt it when the first time you saw me you slipped a wedding band on my finger?" His gibe stung. "So, I make you tense?"

He had a bad way of pulling her back into conversations she preferred to stay away from. "Forget it." She gave up the teasing pose and absently scanned the room. "Next week you'll be gone. My grandparents will be gone. I'll be as calm as a toad in the sunshine."

"That's very picturesque."

Sally avoided looking into his bright blue indignant eyes and watched Myra return with a tray. She placed a mug of steamy coffee before Noah, then set Sally's ice cream and mug before her. "Need anything else?" she asked, her eyes only for Noah. Sally felt invisible.

"That's it," he said.

The waitress laid a ticket beside his mug and leaned over to murmur near his ear. "My number's on the back, cowboy."

Her statement was loud enough for Sally to hear. She couldn't believe the waitress's brazenness. "Of all the…" After Myra wiggled off, Sally frowned at Noah. "Maybe she thinks outlandish flattery will get her a bigger tip."

He flicked her a quick, narrow look, but didn't say anything. Sally knew, deep in her heart, Myra didn't care a fig about a bigger tip. It was Noah she was interested in. He took a sip of his coffee and casually turned over the ticket. There for them both to read was a telephone number. Sally watched his face for reaction as she took a bite of ice cream. She couldn't see any change at all. He just stared, almost seeming as though he were looking through it.

Funny, tonight her peachy treat tasted like wallpaper paste.

Flipping the ticket back over, Noah pulled his wallet from his hip pocket and harvested several bills from the crop of green.

"I've been meaning to ask how you got into metal art," he said, startling her with his choice of subject matter. She supposed she didn't blame him for wanting to focus on something besides how tense he made her.

She swallowed the strangely tasteless ice cream and shrugged. "Daddy had an interest in it. When Mom and Dad bought the old farm with that barn, Dad turned it into a studio. He messed around with it as a hobby and as a little girl I watched, then when I was big enough, I joined in. I loved it."

"You're very good," he said, his expression sincere. The sight did wild and unruly things to her heart.

"Thank you."

His lips crooked in a half grin that didn't quite make it to his eyes. "I don't find fault with everything you do, Sally."

Though the statement was made quietly, she felt the slap in his observation. The accusation she'd made about him finding fault with everything she did had been unfair and untrue. Chastised, she lowered her gaze and took another bite.

"Are those trophies in the studio your dad's then?"

She took another bite and shook her head. When she swallowed, she said, "Mine. High school soccer and track. A couple are bowling trophies." She peered at him through her lashes. "I was on a championship team in the Humble bowling league."

"Humble bowling league," he said with a wry chuckle.

"Hello? Humble, Texas. The town just south of where I live."

He took a sip of his coffee. "Sally Johnson, just north of Humble. Works for me."

She couldn't decide if that was a compliment or a crack. "What do you mean by that?"

"I mean you're no shrinking violet." He set his mug on the table. "And I apologize for assuming the trophies were your father's. It was biased and chauvinistic."

Why was it that the man could ping-pong her back and forth from giddy to grumpy to giddy to grumpy in any given minute? She didn't know what to say, *thank you* or *so there!* She filled the gap by eating her ice cream and scanning the room. Time passed, long, strained strands of time, filled with strident rock music, the buzz of voices and clanks of utensils against pottery. All the seeming normalcy was stressful. Why couldn't anything be routine with Noah around? She usually got a big kick out of her peach ice cream and people-watching.

"Ready to go?" he asked.

She hadn't realized she'd finished her dessert and was absently sipping her coffee. She blinked as she came back to reality, but didn't want to appear as though she hadn't been paying attention to what she was doing. "In a second."

Myra came by. "Refill, babe?"

He shook his head and so did Sally; for all the good it did. Myra didn't bother to turn in her direction. When the smitten waitress was out of hearing range, Sally had to ask, "Did you memorize it?"

He glanced her way, looking puzzled. "Did I memorize what?"

She made a don't-be-dense face, eyed the ticket, then stared at him again. "You know what."

He quirked her a half grin, less humor than disbelief. Even the minimal show of teeth had a scary effect on her heart. "I already have a girlfriend and a wife. Do you think I'm a glutton?"

She slapped down her empty mug. "Her number was 555-7483."

"Two."

"What?"

"The last number was a two, not a three, but thanks." He stood and moved to her side, laying his hand on the back of her chair.

"You *did* memorize it!" She had no idea why she experienced a surge of jealousy. She had no right to. He pulled her chair out for her. "You don't have to act like my wife," he whispered. "Your grandparents are nowhere near here."

She didn't, of course. He was right. Avoiding his eyes, she stood and brushed imaginary wrinkles out of her dress. "Well—as you said, you *do* have a girlfriend," she reminded, lamely. "Besides, if Myra's a day over sixteen I'll—I'll…"

"Don't make any rash promises," he cautioned. "Even if she weren't jailbait, sixteen-year-old girls with green and purple hair aren't my type. I have a good memory for numbers. It's a curse." He took her hand. "As for my girlfriend—" He paused, his brow wrinkling. "Just a second." Withdrawing a small, black device from his pocket he checked it, his furrowed brow turning into a full-fledged frown of concern.

"What is it?"

"My beeper. I called the hospital to let them know I'm in town, in case of an emergency."

"Emergency?"

He nodded, replacing the beeper in his pocket. "Come on." He took her hand. "My cell phone's in the truck."

CHAPTER NINE

NOAH stripped off his surgical gloves, mask and cap. The preemie was alive, thank heaven, and had been transferred to the hospital's top-notch neonatal section. The young mother had almost bled out before she'd managed to hitch a ride to the hospital. The whole procedure was touch-and-go, but she, too, was alive, stable and recovering.

After splashing cold water on his face, Noah grabbed a fresh towel and dried off. He caught sight of his unhappy grimace staring back at him in the mirror. Why was he so blasted miserable? He'd just helped save two fragile lives. A fourteen-year-old mother who'd been kicked out of her house for getting pregnant. A frightened, undernourished girl, so naive, she believed the boy when he'd said he loved her and wanted to marry her, but who was now a bitter memory, long gone from both Texas and her wretched, solitary life.

Noah saw this kind of thing all too often at the free clinic where he volunteered one day a week. Tossing the towel into the hospital hamper he exhaled wearily. He hurt for the young girl, with no one to go to for support. He was angry with the parents who had turned her away. Angry with the teenage boy and his parents who washed their hands of the girl and her pregnancy when a job transfer moved them out of state.

He hoped young Jonetta would give up her firstborn

son for adoption. Give the baby a secure start, and allow Jonetta a second chance at a normal growing up. Allow her to be *just* a teenager and schoolgirl. Let her mature and one day marry some solid citizen who loved her, so next time, when she took on the difficult job of motherhood she would do it with the stability of a second, strong pair of willing hands.

Wishing that for Jonetta and young girls like her wasn't old-fashioned chauvinistic thinking. It was wanting better for her. Raising children today took two salaries and two committed parents. It wasn't a job for a fourteen-year-old child with an inadequate diet and meager lifestyle to take on alone.

He leaned on the sink, head down, his soul aching for the young innocents he cared for in his practice, little more than babies themselves. He damned the men and boys who used them and tossed them aside. Shaking his head, he once again prayed Jonetta would see the benefit for both herself and her baby to give him up to some couple, ready and waiting for a child.

He straightened, then rolled his shoulders to work out the stiffness. He needed to get changed. Sally had been sitting in the maternity waiting room for hours. As he stripped off his hospital greens and showered, he thought about her. He'd been pretty hard on her, heaping his bias against single-motherhood on her head.

When it came right down to it, Sally was a salty, responsible person. She was talented at her art, and clearly made a living at it. If he were any judge, she would one day be renowned. Having seen samples of her work he felt sure once word spread of her talent for hand-crafting high-end architectural features, people would clamor to have her elegant creations in their expensive custom homes. There were plenty of wealthy people in Texas, alone, to keep her creating for decades.

He found himself thinking back on those trophies in her studio: track, soccer *and* bowling. Every day he spent around Sally, he became more and more aware she didn't need anyone's help in any aspect of her life. His most recent discovery—she could outathlete most daddies. "You're quite a woman," he murmured.

"If you're talking to me, Barrett," a gravelly voice called out. "I need a haircut worse than I thought."

Noah recognized the shouter as a fellow doctor and ducked out from under the spray. "I wasn't talking to you, Butch, but a haircut wouldn't do you any harm."

A guttural laugh echoed in the male physician's shower room. "Congratulations on the touchy surgery," Butch said. "I hear both mother and baby are doing fine."

"Thanks. She was lucky she got here when she did." Noah stepped back under the spray. It was time to get off his fixation with little Miss I-Don't-Need-A-Husband. Maybe she didn't. Maybe she was the exception that proved the rule. "Maybe I should get off her back."

"Are you talking to—"

"*No!*" Noah was exasperated with himself. Why this unusual preoccupation over Sally Johnson? Especially since she made it clear she lived for the moment the marriage subterfuge could end and he would vacate her bed—*house*.

*   *   *

Noah didn't say much about the emergency cesarean or the young mother and baby whose lives he'd saved tonight. Sally supposed it was all in a day's work for him—saving lives. But it wasn't for her. She sat in her old rocking chair in the bedroom, reading. Though it was late, she wasn't able to sleep. Noah was in bed, his back to her. Since the rocker sat on the far side of the bed, she hoped the light wouldn't bother him. It didn't seem to. He looked dead to the world. Evidently saving lives took a lot out of a person.

After several false starts, she faced the fact she couldn't concentrate on the book. Her gaze kept trailing to Noah's back, the illumination from her floor lamp highlighting muscle that was very male and alluring.

Even in the relative dimness, his tousled hair gleamed. Clean and soft and cruelly enticing. She itched to touch it, to run her fingers through it, luxuriating in the thickness and texture. She relived the pleasure of his scent, fresh from the shower at the hospital, clean, like soap.

Her mind trailed back to visions of Noah as he came out of surgery in his hospital greens and cap. He gave her a wave as he pulled down his mask. He'd mouthed, ''I'll just be a little longer.'' It was sweet the way he thought of her amid all the rush and trauma.

As she'd sat and waited, she hadn't been able to avoid noticing the nurses whispering about the handsome, dashing doctor and the dicey procedure. It was clear from their smiles and hidden glances as he passed in the corridor, more than one would be happy to trade places with her—and not just pretending, either.

A strong kick from Vivica brought Sally back to the present. She was shocked to see her paperback book fly out of her hands. In an odd slow motion she watched the novel arc into the air, sailing over the bed, to strike directly between Noah's shoulder blades.

"What the..." He rolled to his back and peered at her, blue eyes narrowed either in annoyance or because of the light. "If you want my attention, calling my name works great."

She sat exactly as she was when her novel flew out of her hands. Her fingers were curled around empty air that no longer contained the book. The only change was that her mouth had dropped open in surprise.

"I—I didn't throw the book." Hearing her own voice seemed to release her from her paralysis, and she spread her hands over her belly. "Vivica did it." She smiled at the wild party her daughter was having. "She's kicking up a storm. Come feel."

Noah hesitated for a second, looking surprised by the offer. She was a little surprised, herself. But she didn't take it back. After the brief delay, Noah tossed back the covers and padded around the bed. He looked tall and ruggedly sexy, wearing nothing more than a pair of striped shorts. The window was open to the chilly night breeze, and Sally wondered how he could stand it. She still wore her flannel gown and terry robe.

As he knelt beside her rocking chair she began to rethink her offer. All that tempting, male flesh so near. "You're suggesting your daughter kicked that book so hard it flew all the way across the bed and hit me?" His expression was a charming mix of skepticism and amusement.

Sally couldn't help grinning at Vivica's late-night antics. "Well, it wasn't me." She nodded toward her stomach. "Go ahead. Check for yourself."

She lifted one hand away from her stomach and coaxed his fingers from the arm of the rocker, pressing his hand where hers had been. Vivica obliged by giving his palm a good wallop.

"Whoa." He laughed. "I predict she'll be the first female placekicker for the Dallas Cowboys football team."

"Not hardly. She'll be an astronaut."

His hand heated her skin, even through the layers of the fabric.

"What a waste of a good kicker," he kidded.

She made a face. "My daughter will be a brilliant scientist *and* philosopher."

"Is that all?" he asked, a brow lifting skeptically.

He was making fun. He probably heard mothers-to-be making grandiose claims about their prenatal prodigies every day. Undaunted, she lifted her chin, "No, that's not all. She'll also be a famous artist."

"I don't doubt that."

There was something in his tone, something absolutely sincere, so much so that she could only stare into those mirror-bright eyes. In the lamplight his gaze seemed to smolder with emotion. She found herself hoping it wasn't a trick of the light.

Slowly her smile died and she swallowed. She could get used to looking at Noah this way, shirtless, his eyes earnest and animated, his big, capable hand caressing her stomach. She swallowed a second time. "Thank you, Noah."

"I'm glad I'm here," he said softly, smiling. He seemed to lean nearer, and Sally had the sense she was going to be kissed. But the thought, the impression, lasted only an instant before he cleared his throat. "That reminds me. I need to set my alarm." Applying slight pressure on her stomach, he gave Vivica an affectionate little squeeze.

"Why?" The question slipped out a little late. She'd actually been asking why he was glad he was there. Her foolish heart hoped for a ridiculous, outrageous and unwise answer—that he might be glad he was spending his vacation with an eccentric, pregnant "welder."

Sure, Sally, sure! Dream on!

"I promised Jonetta I'd drop by the hospital and see her in the morning. She's a scared little girl and she's been through a lot. I'm glad I was able to be with her when she needed me." He stood. "You should get to sleep." He indicated her book, lying squarely in his place on the bed. "I think Vivica wants you to quit reading for tonight."

Sally didn't appreciate being talked to like a child, especially by Noah. She preferred not to analyze whether her quick flush of anger was due to the fact he was glad he was in Houston because of his young patient, instead of her. "Gee, thanks, Doctor!" she said, sarcastically. "What would I do without your *unsolicited* advice?"

The next day brought a pleasant surprise. Hubert sat up. He sat up to eat, and by evening was complaining of being very bored. Some way, Sally wasn't sure how, she found herself sitting beside his bed with a bridge hand clutched to her breast. Noah, her partner, sat across from her. Abigail, Hubert's partner, perched near the foot of the four-poster on Noah's side.

Mrs. Vanderkellen didn't seem very provoked at the

moment. Perhaps it was because she loved bridge almost as much as tramping around pyramid ruins. Sally didn't enjoy the game, much, but she knew how to play. Noah, on the other hand, was extremely good. Possibly even brilliant. No matter what flub she made, he was able to work around and even manage to continually win.

Sally wondered if he could possibly be cheating, then discarded the idea as ridiculous. She played her hands as well as she could and marveled at Noah's easy, charming, ingenious card playing. It was clear no matter how practiced and adept at the game Abigail was, Noah wasn't going to be beaten without extraordinary ability. Sally wondered if her grandmother had it in her.

"Your play, darling."

Sally snapped her gaze to Noah's face. "Oh—right." She scanned the cards in her hand and struggled with her decision. "I'm just so bad at this." She had a thought and glanced at Abigail. "I take after mother where bridge is concerned. She was awful. No matter how Daddy tried, she just couldn't get it." *So there!* She loved her mother, but it was true. Her father was the salty bridge player in their family.

Abigail's features clouded for a moment. She looked sad, so much so that Sally had to turn away. She concentrated on her hand and made a difficult decision. She slapped down a card, giving Noah an apologetic look. "I hope that doesn't mess you up."

He winked, and her toes curled. There were times when his playacting was too real for her mental health. She felt a blush creep into her cheeks. Embarrassed, she broke eye contact and looked at her grandfather. He was dummy, so he sat there with his arms crossed over his belly, eyeing his wife. "So play," he said, looking irked. "And it'd better be good. They doubled you, you know."

"Hush!" she said, thumbing her cards. "If you'd had what your bid said you had I wouldn't be having so much trouble now!"

Hubert rolled his eyes and reached for a glass of water on the side table muttering something about never playing with her again. Sally had a feeling he'd muttered the same threat a million times over the years.

Abigail played her card and gave Noah a serious look, obviously trying to see into his brain. Sally looked at him, too, but couldn't tell anything. He was not only good at bridge, but he had a great poker face.

After a second, Noah said, "Abigail, you sly thing, you almost had me believing you could make that four hearts bid, even doubled. But…" He arched an eyebrow to emphasize the pause, then laid his remaining cards on hers. "I think I have the rest. If you'd prefer, we can play it out."

Abigail eyed his cards for a few seconds, checked her own, then let out a wail of defeat. Hubert harrumphed, thumping his water glass down.

Abigail surprised Sally when she reached over and gave Noah's hand a pat. "Marvelous game, son. For someone living in these rustic backwoods, you play remarkably well."

Sally watched Noah's face to see how he would take her backhanded compliment. He merely smiled. "Thank you, Grandmother." He gathered the cards from the quilt that covered Hubert's legs and began to shuffle. "Bridge was a required course in my family. Are you up for another battering?"

"Oh, please, no," Sally said, with a yawn. "It's after eleven. Vivica and I are pooped."

Noah quit shuffling and gathered the cards in a deck. "Of course, sugarplum." He handed the cards to Hubert. "You and Abigail play gin." He stood and walked around the bed to assist Sally from her chair. "Good night, Grandmother, Grandfather." He placed a husbandly arm around Sally's shoulders and squeezed, the picture of an affectionate mate. "Hubert, how's that back?"

The older man made a face. "Fair. Only fair. I figure another day or so and I'll be able to walk—a little."

Abigail's snort of contempt was utterly unaristocratic. "*A little* walking around a St. Martin golf course you mean, you old faker."

"Now, Abigail, snookums, don't be like that," Hubert whined. "I'm a man in pain."

Sally and Noah left the room, closing the door on whatever rejoinder Abigail threw back about her husband's malingering.

Sally shook her head at her grandparents' behavior. "They are amazing. How they've stayed married for five thousand years is beyond me."

"I think they're funny."

"Funny?" she echoed with disbelief. "How can you say that, of all people?" she asked as they went into their room. "Grandmother keeps zinging you with those insults." Noah's arm still encircled her shoulders. She could step out of his embrace now that they were behind closed doors, but for some reason she didn't. "I'd love to see her face if she knew she was being rude to a Boston Barrett.''

"Sally, you place too much importance on such things," he said, finally slipping his arm from around her. The room seemed suddenly cold.

"No! They're the ones who place the importance on such things! That's the point. I'd like my grandmother to be snubbed and looked down on. Let her know what it feels like—*once in her life!*"

Facing her he slid his hands to her shoulders. Their pressure was light and gentle. "You have to get over this anger you feel for your grandparents. It's—"

"What would you know about it?" she cut in, cross with his everlasting I'm-right-you're-wrong viewpoint, however softly spoken. She poked his shirtfront. "What exactly would you, a high-and-mighty doctor *and* a Boston Barrett, know about it, huh? Have you ever been assured by word and deed that you were unworthy of your own grandparents' time?" With the flats of her hands on his chest, she shoved. "Just stay out of my personal business."

"You dragged me into it," he reminded her, his eyes taking on an affronted glint. "Besides, being a Boston Barrett isn't all it's cracked up to be."

"Oh, yeah?" she jeered. "Just how is it not?"

He shrugged and walked away to sit on the edge of the bed. It creaked with his weight. "For one thing, you don't know if people are with you because you're you or just to be associated with the Barrett name."

She glared at him, her fists plunked on her hips. "Poor baby. Saddled with the hardship of being the cream of Boston society. My heart bleeds for you!"

He eyed her sternly. "The stigma even reaches all the way to Texas." He indicated her with a curt wave. "You're prejudiced against me because my name is Barrett."

"Ha! Any negative vibrations I feel for you are well-earned," she spat. "From the day we met, you've told me I'm selfish, shortsighted and ill prepared to bring up a child alone. Now you're telling me I'm overreacting to the despicable way my grandparents behaved toward their own daughter and her family. If that's your idea of sweet talk, no wonder you're still single."

For a long moment he didn't speak, and she didn't, either, though a little voice inside her head kept whining something about how mean-spirited and overwrought her retort had been.

He leaned forward, resting his hands on his knees. "I'm sorry," he murmured.

She couldn't believe what she thought she'd heard. "Huh?"

His features grim, he met her gaze. "I said, I'm sorry. You're as well equipped to raise a child as any single mother I know."

She took in his solemn comment then rolled it around in her brain, picking it apart, checking for traps and tricks. At last, she decided she'd found the loophole, and shot him a twisted smirk. "That's what's called damning with faint praise, right?"

He aimed those serious, sexy baby blues at her for another heartbeat before his lips tilted in a grin every bit as twisted and cynical as hers. "Yeah. Sure."

CHAPTER TEN

NOAH returned from the hospital, where Jonetta and her baby were doing well. He also had good news from the young mother. She'd decided to give up her son for adoption. The chosen couple, who had been waiting for over three years, had already rushed to the hospital to see their baby. Noah met them and liked them immediately. They were both crying tears of joy as they gazed at their preemie through the glass.

The instant Noah stepped inside Sally's front door, the phone in the entryway started ringing. He checked his watch. Ten-thirty. Sally would be in her studio working on Vivica's crib. He picked up the receiver. The caller identified himself as an architect, and said his clients had agreed to Sally's price for the custom staircase banister. When could they meet and discuss details? Noah took the message and a number and said he'd relay the information.

As he hung up, he heard the back porch screen door bang shut. "Sally?"

"Yes?"

He ripped the page off the telephone pad and took it to the kitchen. "You had a call."

She wore maternity overalls and a pink, knit turtleneck. Her cheeks were as bright as the shirt from the hot work. Wet strands of blond hair framed her flushed face. She took the note. Glancing at it, she grabbed a glass

154

from a cabinet and filled it with tap water, then drained it with a few, long gulps.

"That's a lot of money," Noah said, impressed with the sum she could command.

She sat the glass on the countertop and inhaled. "It's a six-month job." She looked at him as though daring him to suggest she was overcharging. "How much do you make in six months?"

He felt the jab of her query. He did make more than that, if that's what she was trying to point out. Shaking his head, he walked to the table and placed his hands on the back of a chair. "I wasn't suggesting you were charging too much." He didn't know why, but he couldn't seem to say anything she didn't take as an insult. What was the problem? He was usually good at getting along with people. He tried again. "I was suggesting you can command hefty prices, so your work must be highly regarded."

She lounged against the counter, spreading her hands over the baby she carried. She looked at him, skepticism darkening her expression. After a minute, she blew a puff of air upward, setting some of the errant strands in her eyes to fluttering. "Oh." She shrugged as though accepting the possibility he might be complimenting her. "Actually, it's not such a hefty price. But, I make a living."

He pondered that. "It should be."

She looked at him, her eyes narrowing. "What does that mean?"

There she went again, assuming the worst. He leaned on the chair-back. "I mean, you should charge what would be considered a hefty price, because you're *that* good.''

She watched him for a long minute, as though trying to read his mind. After what felt like a year, she took a deep breath and pushed away from the counter. ''Thanks.'' Breaking eye contact, she turned toward the door to the hallway. ''I guess I'll go call and set up that appointment.''

She breezed past Noah, her attention focused on the exit. After she was gone, he poured himself a cup of coffee and sat down at the table. He could hear her on the phone but couldn't make out the words.

She laughed at something. The sound was light and breezy and too unfamiliar. The lilting warmth of it, the musical quality, curled, soft and sexy, around Noah's heart and squeezed.

Sally was having a hard day. She'd spent the afternoon in her studio, working on Vivica's crib, not only because she would be needing it in just a few weeks, but because she was thinking troubling thoughts. Noah's latest compliment stayed with her. He seemed truly impressed by her artistry. He seemed to actually think her creations were valuable, and by working with iron, she didn't automatically dwell on some lower social class than he.

Noah might be a doctor, but he held little resemblance to her stuffy, social-climbing ex-fiancé. And Noah also held little resemblance to her impression of the Boston Barretts. He cared deeply for his indigent single mothers, like Jonetta and her newborn. He wasn't a snob. On the whole, Noah was a sensitive, caring man. She even had to admit that he *might* have a right to his feelings about single motherhood. After all, he did have firsthand knowledge of the subject, and no doubt knew of many sad cases.

And she mustn't forget that he'd done her a great favor by sacrificing a week of his vacation with his girl-friend to help in a ploy she now realized had been stupid and unnecessary. What did it matter if the Vanderkellens approved of her or if she showed them how wrong they'd been about her wonderful father? He was still wonderful whether they believed it or not. Plus, her decision to become a mother was her business, and whether she was married or not was likewise nobody's business but hers.

She didn't quite know how, but Noah had helped her see that, too. Maybe it was the way he behaved around them all. He was just himself. He didn't flaunt his Barrettness or his doctorness. He'd been accommodating and helpful and, though he could rile her with his advice and opinions, he had a right to express them, especially considering she'd dragged him into her farce. Not many men would have stuck it out for seven days and nights. After all, "lover girl" was all suntanned and supine and waiting in the wings.

Sally experienced a jealous twinge, and tried not to think about it. Noah's love life should be the least of her concerns. She was about to give birth, for heaven's sake! She was about to become a mother. A parent, *responsible* for a human life. Any lustful fantasies had to be squelched. Especially since the object of that lust had a love interest of his own.

She wiped sweat from her forehead. The studio was hot, and she'd put in a long day. She stood at a special area on her worktable, using a bending fork to shape a forged bar, wedged between two one-and-one-half-inch pins. The final support for her nearly completed crib bent as she applied pressure.

Her gaze lifted to rove over the lacy filigree of twisted and curled ironwork sitting on the worktable. Reminiscent of ribbons and lace, intertwined and tossed by a capricious breeze, the delicate, ethereal piece would soon be the crib Sally would place her baby daughter in when they returned from the hospital.

She finished shaping the leg and smiled at her handiwork. "It'll be a wonderful bed, sweetie." She lay aside the bending fork and patted her tummy. "Only the best for my little girl."

"Sally?"

Hearing her name spoken by her grandmother's Boston-tainted accent made Sally jump. She hadn't heard the door, since it stood ajar to let in cool early-evening air.

She turned, frowned. "Is something wrong?"

Abigail walked in, clearly tentative around the machinery. Sally guessed her grandmother looked every bit as ill at ease when she went to the Mercedes garage to fetch her car after a tune-up. No doubt she was afraid she'd get soot on her gray silk dress and matching kid pumps.

Abigail's glance fell on the crib and she continued to look at it as she approached the worktable. "No—nothing's wrong. Noah sent me to tell you dinner is ready."

Sally experienced another twinge and couldn't tell if it was guilt or longing. He'd fixed dinner. She must find a way to make all this up to him. Maybe he'd like a wrought-iron gate or bench. She must remember to make the offer. "Oh. Thanks." She took off her gloves and lay them aside. "I'm just finishing for the day." She removed her baseball cap and laid it beside the gloves. "I'll be right in."

Sally turned away to untie her heavy apron. When Abigail didn't respond, she glanced at her grandmother. "Is there something else?" She couldn't imagine what the older woman's uneasy expression might mean. She was probably thinking all manner of "welder" type things Sally didn't want to know.

"I—I was wondering…" She clasped her hands together, looking nervous. "I was wondering, Sally, if you might consider allowing Hubert and me to be a part of your daughter's life?" She looked away for an instant, as though gathering herself, then resumed eye contact. "I realize we don't deserve to be, that we've earned your dislike, but…" She swallowed and cleared her throat. "But it would mean a great deal to us."

Sally stared at her grandmother, her emotions roiling. They most certainly *had* earned her dislike! And they most certainly did *not* deserve to be a part of Vivica's life! How dare they just drop in one afternoon, coerce her to put them up for a week, then ask that they be allowed into her daughter's life? She glared, not quite knowing how to voice her total abhorrence, her complete rejection, of the request. She started to tell Abigail an unqualified *no way,* but she couldn't find her voice.

How many times in her growing-up years had she fantasized about her longed-for grandparents begging to be with her and then she'd soundly rejected them? What was her problem now? Where was the scathing rebuke she'd imagined angrily spewing so many, many times in her daydreams?

After a couple of failed attempts to tell her grand-mother exactly where she could take her request, Sally saw Abigail shake her head and wave off any answer. "Of course, of course. I understand your feelings. You have every right to despise us." She took in a breath, plainly attempting to hold on to her composure. She indicated the cradle. "That is quite lovely." Facing her granddaughter once again, she said, "I would very much like to commission a piece of your work, Sally. As you know we're having our Boston home redone. Would you consider it? On a strictly business basis, naturally. We wouldn't expect a family rate. Hubert and I would be—extremely grateful to own one of your creations. You are extraordinarily talented."

"I get my artistic talent from my father," she said, shoulders back, chin jutted.

Abigail seemed to deflate, clearly pricked by the cutting remark. Her gaze plummeted to her bejeweled hands, clutched tightly together. "He—he must have been a fine person." She glanced back at Sally, her expression forlorn. "You will be happy to know Hubert has been out of bed, walking. I've checked on flights. We can leave tonight and meet our cruise ship on St. Martin. You and Noah have been more than generous to—" her voice broke, but she didn't break eye contact "—to us. We'll leave right after dinner."

She turned away and without another word, left the studio.

Sally's righteous anger slowly dissipated, leaving uncertainty in its place. Had her grandmother actually said what it sounded like? They were leaving?

Tonight?

She stared at the open doorway, tormented by a rush of conflicting emotions. If they were going—then Noah was leaving, too.

True to the fraud, Sally and Noah accompanied the Vanderkellens to the airport. The ride in her midsize sedan was made in tense silence, but for the few times Noah attempted conversation. Sally blessed him for trying to ease the tension. She didn't have it in her. Too much was going through her mind, too many emotions battling for superiority.

She was glad to see her grandparents go. So why did the farewell trip prey so heavily on her soul? Why wasn't she chattering happily away? Why did she keep seeing Abigail's sad face in her mind's eye, when she asked to be a part of little Vivica's life? Why? Hubert and Abigail had earned their place *outside* Sally's life. Why should she consider for one second sharing her baby with them?

Standing at the departure gate, Sally chewed her lower lip as Noah wished her grandparents a good trip. It was a small, commuter plane, so there were only a handful of passengers waiting to board.

When the flight was called, Noah shook Hubert's hand and gave Abigail a son-in-lawish peck on the cheek. Sally's eyes met Abigail's, and she was horrified to see moisture glistening there. Lord, her grandmother was near tears. Something inside Sally broke into little pieces. Maybe it was the hard-fought barrier she'd built up over the years to protect herself from the disregard and disdain of these snobbish, selfish strangers who were her grandparents.

But suddenly they weren't strangers any longer, and she could see pain and regret in her grandmother's eyes. Eyes the image of her own mother's. Even Hubert looked smaller and frailer, his expression crestfallen as he said goodbye.

They had been wrong so long ago when they turned their backs on their only daughter. Sally could see in their faces how much they had paid for their mistake— with long, joyless years of estrangement. In their stiff-backed, pitiful way, they were asking for forgiveness, for a chance to reconnect.

Without allowing herself time to reconsider the wisdom of her act, she lunged forward and embraced her grandmother. ''Goodbye,'' she said, her voice rough with emotion. ''I'll call you after the baby's born.'' She moved swiftly away to give her grandfather a brief, hard hug. ''Have a good trip and take care of that back.''

When she released him, she paused only long enough to blink back tears before she grabbed Noah's hand and tugged him away with her. After hurrying fifty paces down the corridor, she looked back. They were no longer there, having been herded along with the others onto the plane.

''Well, well,'' Noah said. ''That was nice.''

She wiped at a tear with the back of her hand. ''It was weak.''

''Weak?''

She sniffed. ''Apparently I don't have the courage of my convictions.''

He squeezed her hand, pulling her to a halt. "You have courage, Sally." He pulled her to face him. "And you showed a great deal of class." He slung an arm around her shoulders. "But there's one thing I have to ask."

She sniffed again, getting herself under control. His soft compliment had helped ease her sadness. "What's that?"

"What will you tell them about me?"

She glanced his way. "Oh."

He lifted a brow. "Oh, is right. Suddenly we're not deliriously happy any longer? And jerk that I am, I left you before the baby was born?"

She heaved a sigh. "I'll tell them the truth."

"About the artificial insemination?"

"Yes. After all Grandmother had the same female problem as mother did and most of the rest of the family."

"But not you?"

She peered sideways at him. "Well—not yet, but I don't want to be caught unprepared."

He grinned. "I don't see that ever happening."

Another compliment? She watched him for a moment, then, breaking eye contact, she murmured, "Thanks."

They walked to the car sharing a companionable silence. It was an unexpected, but nice interlude. On the way home he broke the stillness, asking, "Are you going to tell them I'm not Noah Step but Noah Barrett?"

She thought about that for a minute. "Probably not."

He glanced her way. "And miss the chance to see your grandmother's face?"

She lay back against the headrest and exhaled, very

weary. "I guess." Then she looked at him. "What's funny?"

"Nothing." He glanced her way, his smile warming her insides. "Just, thanks for not using me."

She was confused. "But I did use you—for a week."

He shook his head. "No, I mean—the Barrett thing."

She realized what he meant and smiled, though a heaviness in her heart made the expression difficult. "You're welcome. Anytime."

She experienced a painful contraction and winced. *Oh fine, another bout of false labor.* Closing her eyes she endured the crushing sensation in silence and concentrated on the pleasantness of Noah's scent.

Tomorrow he would catch his flight to Aruba. She bit the inside of her cheek as the contraction continued to cinch her middle.

Right now she preferred not to think about her body "practicing" or about Noah's departure from her life. She inhaled his redolence and allowed herself the crazy, lovely fantasy that little Vivica would come into the world with two parents—Noah Barrett filling the real-life part as her daddy.

"Are you okay?" he asked.

The sound of his voice was nice, too. Deep and rich. She could listen to him for the rest of her life. She nodded. "As well as can be expected," she said, without opening her eyes. Even with false labor pains slashing at her middle, she knew she would hold in her heart the memory of this last drive home with Noah, for a long, long time.

She refused to allow the word love into her head,

though it pounded and shouted and made a nuisance of itself. She couldn't allow it entry. If she did, she feared it would cause her a deep, agonizing pain she would not be able to endure.

CHAPTER ELEVEN

SALLY recalled vividly how she'd snapped at Noah, assuring him she would never bother him again with her false labor pains. Unfortunately it was starting to look like these supposedly "practice" pains weren't false. She'd been timing her contractions for the past two hours, and they'd begun to be alarmingly regular and only about five minutes apart.

She lay on her side in bed, surrounded by pillows, all alone. Since there was no need for the pretense any longer, Noah had gathered up his things and moved into the room where her grandparents had slept. There hadn't even been any discussion about it. As Sally lay there, she tried not to feel abandoned. How foolish could she be?

Since she was timing the contractions, she'd left on the bedside light so she could see her wristwatch. The hour hand pointed to the three, the minute to the six. The second hand trudged agonizingly slowly around the face as Sally endured the strong contraction. She knew from her classes and reading on the subject that pains this regular and close together were a sign that real labor had started. She chewed her lip with uncertainty. Could Vivica really be planning to make her appearance three weeks early? She supposed these things happened, even with a first baby.

After a few more minutes of vacillation, she made her

decision and struggled up to sit. She'd better give her doctor a call and see if he thought he should meet her at the hospital. She pushed off the bed and slipped on her robe. A new contraction gripped her in a vise of pain. She closed her eyes and held onto the metal footboard until the worst of it passed. Sliding on her scuffs, she headed out of her room.

After slowly lumbering down the stairs, she grabbed up the phone and called her doctor's answering service, explaining her situation. She was told to stand by. Her doctor would call her back. She stood in the entryway, waiting. It couldn't have been more than a minute, but it seemed like forever.

The phone rang and she nabbed the receiver. "Hello, Dr. Plattan?"

She described her symptoms and her doctor told her to get to the hospital. When she hung up she started for the stairs to wake Noah, but it wasn't necessary. He loomed at the top of the staircase. "You're in labor?" he asked, tucking his shirttail into a pair of jeans.

She was startled by his appearance and apparent psychic ability. "Uh—yes. I could be. My doctor thinks I should head for the hospital." She made a face when another contraction crushed her middle. "I need to change," she said, her voice gruff with pain.

Noah came quickly down the steps, his boots resounding on the wood. "Is your overnight case in the car?"

She nodded.

"Then let's go." He swooped her into his arms. "I can bring you a change of clothes to wear home on my way to the airport, tomorrow."

She wasn't in any shape to argue. Her energy was

focused on breathing to relieve the unmerciful grip of pain.

Sally found herself gently placed in the passenger's seat of her car. Noah strode around the hood and slid in behind the wheel. She was grateful he was there. Getting a taxi way out here in the boondocks would have been a delay she might not have had time for. She sensed the baby wasn't planning to wait long to be born.

"How are you?" Noah asked.

"I think I'm going to have a baby," she gritted out.

Wearing a concerned frown, he pulled out of the gravel driveway onto the country road, heading toward the highway. "Has your water broken?"

"No." She peered his way. "I'd just as soon it didn't until we get there. So don't give it any ideas."

He didn't look at her as he sped along the curvy blacktop. "Don't worry. I'll get you there. But if you decide to deliver on the way, remember, I'm a doctor."

She leaned back. Trying to relax, she kept her eyes shut. "Just concentrate on getting there."

"What in the…"

Noah's incomplete query caused Sally some concern and she opened her eyes. "What?"

As he slowed he indicated ahead. "It looks like a roadblock."

Sally squinted forward. A black-and-white DPS Highway Patrol car half blocked the road, its red and blue roof lights flashed, evidence that something was not right beyond the turnoff ahead.

The Highway Patrol Trooper waved a flashlight, indicating that they halt. Noah rolled down his window. "What's the problem? I have a pregnant woman here."

The trooper bent to check the interior of the car. Sally gave him a wan smile, then cringed with a new contraction.

"Sorry, sir. Ma'am." He put a finger to his Western-style hat brim in a brief, polite salute, then indicated ahead with his flashlight. "Accident on the highway. Cattle truck overturned. Nearly a hundred heads running all over," he explained in his unhurried drawl. "Traffic's backed up for miles. There's no way you all'd get anyplace for a couple hours." He looked worriedly at Sally. "I don't know, ma'am. Maybe you could get the hospital emergency chopper. It'd be the only way."

With a nod of understanding, Noah turned the car around and headed back to Sally's house.

"What—now?" she asked.

He gave her a look that was part sympathetic and part determination. "We're going to have a baby."

"We are?" She didn't like the "we." The idea of Noah delivering Vivica was too—too intimate a thing for him to do with her. Her groan was only partly due to the contraction ripping at her. "You *are* going to call for the helicopter."

"Don't you trust me?"

She didn't know how to say what she was feeling. "It's not that—it's just—you're not my doctor." That was true, but hardly what was bothering her.

"Sally, the helicopter is for life and death situations. Has your doctor given you any indication your delivery might be anything but normal?"

Should she lie simply to get the helicopter? Did she dare insist on it, when somewhere out there a car accident might happen? The only chance for a poor victim's survival could be lost because of her prudish self-indulgence. No, she couldn't chance being responsible for a tragedy that needn't happen. Sadly, but honestly, she murmured, "Well—no, I guess Dr. Plattan expected everything to be normal."

"Good." Though his expression remained serious, he gave her an encouraging smile. It affected her too much like an aphrodisiac for her current circumstances. "I've delivered hundreds of babies. I promise, I'll get Vivica into this world with all her fingers and toes."

She wasn't worried about that. She sensed Noah was a wonderful doctor. Still, that knowledge didn't calm her one iota. She stirred uneasily in her seat.

They arrived back at her house. He cut the engine, got out of the car and came around to carry her inside. She clung to him, thinking murderous thoughts about every last steer roaming aimlessly on the highway.

"Maybe if we wait a while, we can still make it," she tried, her voice rising in panic.

He shouldered through the door. "You'd better check with Vivica. She may have other plans."

Before Sally knew it, Noah whisked her up to the wrought-iron bed and settled her in.

"Hang on while I get some towels."

She started to object to this whole having-a-baby-with-Noah idea, but a new, excruciating contraction took her breath and she moaned. "Breathe," she told herself. "You know the drill. Breathe."

When he came back he pulled the rocking chair up to the side of the bed and took her hand, his touch snagging her attention. She peered at him.

"I called your doctor and told her the situation."

"What did she say?" Sally asked though gritted teeth, hoping against hope her doctor had insisted they call for the helicopter.

Noah's smile was gentle, compassionate. "She said to give Vivica a kiss for her."

Sally closed her eyes and moaned. *It's a conspiracy!*

"This birth is going to be totally natural," Noah said. "I don't have anything to ease your pain."

She frowned at him. "You could hit me with a chair."

His features were serious, tender. "Remember those relaxing exercises?"

She nodded, scrunching her eyes shut.

"And how impeccable you are at them?"

She had said that, hadn't she.

"This would be a good time to show off." He smoothed damp hair out of her face. Even in her pain, Sally experienced a wayward tingle of desire at his touch.

"You ask a lot," she said, but she knew he was right. What had she been to all those classes for? She knew what to do. Sucking in a breath, she nodded. "Okay."

He smiled, and she felt it all the way to her toes. She saw warmth and—even admiration glistening in the blue depths. It was quite a sight to behold. Breathtaking and heart-pounding. And the most miraculous thing about it was—it wasn't an act. The very idea that Noah would, could—well, those eyes, that softly caressing look, cut her pain level in half. That's how powerful the effect was.

Sally never would have believed that in a time so brief as one, short week, life could get so complicated. Tomorrow, she would have her beloved daughter,

Vivica, the child she'd wanted so badly, the most precious gift she could imagine.

She should be completely and wholly content. Up until very recently she would have been. All she'd thought she needed was her baby and herself to make a happy family.

Once she held her child, Sally knew she would be delighted. But suddenly and with great clarity, she also knew there would be a gaping rip in her heart that no amount of time, nor love for her child, could heal.

For tomorrow, Noah would be gone.

Sally woke to a lovely, spring day. The sun shone outside her bedroom window and the lace curtains fluttered with a fragrant breeze. She was tired, but filled with joy. Looking down, she saw the tiny little head of her newborn, eyes wide as she stared up at the brand-new world she'd entered sometime before dawn.

Sally kissed the top of her head, covered with a halo of blond, baby fuzz. She took a deep breath, the scent of her child filling her with awe. Her mind drifted back over the hours before dawn with Noah. He had been so gentle, aiding her in the birthing process. Far from being embarrassing, it had all seemed so natural, so right.

Now she knew she would not have had her first child come into the world any other way, or delivered into anyone else's gentle care than Noah's. He'd spoken to her newborn ever so softly, welcoming her into the world. He'd cleaned her, diapered and wrapped her in one of the many receiving blankets Sally had accumulated in her well-stocked nursery.

The most beautiful moment of all had been when he lay her baby daughter in her arms.

Sally had been exhausted, but happy. She would never forget the way Noah kissed little Vivica's forehead. Then, he'd bent to present Sally with a soft kiss that barely brushed the corner of her mouth, as he whispered, "I feel as though I was a part of something very special last night." He left them alone after that, so mother and daughter could bond and get some sleep.

Of course, Noah needed sleep, too. She didn't blame him for going. But she couldn't wait to see him again, to hug him, thank him, tell him he had certainly been part of something special. The experience was awe-inspiring. Vivica's birth, her first spirited cries, Noah's glistening eyes and dazzling, sweet smile. He'd made her daughter's arrival more extraordinary than she would have believed possible.

She yawned and stretched, feeling amazingly well, considering she'd just given birth to an eight-pound baby girl. She shook her head and smiled down at her daughter. "What would you have weighed if you were born when you were supposed to have been, young lady?"

Vivica yawned, her little hands wagging in the air, tiny fingers fisting and unfisting.

Sally heard footsteps in the hallway and her heart fluttered. He was coming. A warm glow enveloped her. She knew now, without reservation, without one single doubt, that her feelings for Noah didn't stem from over-active hormones, as she'd tried to tell herself. No, somewhere in these last seven, harried days, she'd fallen in love with the man she'd shanghaied into her crazy marriage plot. Hugging her baby close, she kissed the top of her downy head. "Do we dare hope he loves us, too?" she whispered. Right now, with her newborn in her arms, anything seemed possible.

She and Noah had been through something extremely intimate, extremely unique, between a man and a woman. Oh, he'd delivered many babies before, but she sensed this had been different for him. She sensed a closeness, an intimacy and—dare she say it? Passion. She'd seen it glistening in his eyes, lighting his smile, heard it in the timbre of his voice. Felt it in his kiss, however chaste. She knew in her heart of hearts Noah felt something very real for her. *He had to!*

A light knock on her door brought her out of her expectant musings. "Noah, come in," she called, her heart rate skyrocketing. "No need for formality, now." She laughed, the sound light, lilting and nervous in her ears.

The door opened, and her laughter abruptly ended. It wasn't Noah at all, but a stranger, a woman in white. "Mrs. Johnson?"

Sally stared. "No—Miss. Who are you?"

The woman came inside and closed the door at her back. The white turned out to be a nurse's uniform. The woman was a graying, robust matron, with wire-rimmed spectacles and a broad, ruby-red smile. "I'm Agnes Himes. Dr. Barrett hired me to help you for a few days." She bustled around the room as she spoke, messing with the curtains and retucking covers. "Would you care for a little breakfast, dear?"

Sally shook her head, more out of confusion than to answer the question. "Where's Noah?"

The nurse stilled, resting one hand lightly on Sally's

forehead. ''Why, he left an hour ago. I believe he said he had a flight to catch.''

Sally's heart dropped, plummeted into a deep dark pit. *The vacation. The long-awaited, long-anticipated getaway with the girlfriend.*

Her gaze clouded and she blinked to fight off tears, amazed at how swiftly a simple statement could cause such raw devastation to her soul. ''Oh. Yes, I'd—I'd forgotten for a minute.''

The nurse straightened and smiled. ''You certainly have a beautiful daughter, Miss Johnson.''

''Thank you,'' she murmured, her great happiness of a moment ago muted by Noah's defection. ''Please, call me Sally.''

''And you call me Agnes, dear.'' She smoothed her pristine uniform. ''You should have some liquids. How about a nice big glass of orange juice?''

Sally nodded, though she wasn't interested in food. If it would get rid of the woman for a few minutes, it was worth it.

''Fine, fine.''

''Maybe some oatmeal, too?'' Sally added, needing time to herself.

''Wonderful. Then I'll help you get started with the basics of feeding of your precious little Vivica.''

Sally could only nod, her throat blocked by a great, ridiculous grief. Noah was gone. He hadn't even stayed around to say goodbye. So much for her fine-feathered notions about how special the event had been for him. So much for seeing anything like passion in his eyes or sensing anything but goodbye in his kiss. Every new mother probably got a little delirious while giving birth. Why should she be different?

The nurse left the room and closed the door. Not a moment too soon, for Sally could no longer contain her tears. Her sorrow became a burning, agonizing knot inside her. Much, much more painful and suffocating than any birthing contraction could ever be.

With a choked sob, she cuddled her baby to her. "Oh, sweetheart—" Her voice broke, and she had to swallow several times before she could go on. "Don't grow up to be a romantic fool like your mama."

CHAPTER TWELVE

SALLY and her daughter were beginning their second week of a brand-new family tradition. Sunday afternoons were set aside for picnics in the front yard under the dogwood trees. Most of the year the dogwoods wouldn't be in bloom as they were today, so the snowy blossoms covering the trees made this afternoon's picnic extra special. Sally sat on the checkered blanket, leaning back on her hands and gazing up at the delicate blooms heralding the arrival of spring. Vivica lay beside her, kicking precious little bare feet.

Vivica made a gurgling sound and Sally gazed down at her daughter and smiled. The infant's wide blue eyes were so intelligent. Sally just knew her baby daughter was aware of the flowering beauty above her, wagging gently in the breeze.

She pressed her index finger against her daughter's palm and giggled as the baby grabbed and held tight. "Not sleepy yet, punkin?" Little Vivica had already had her lunch, so she would be asleep in a short while. In the meantime, Sally loved watching her daughter's fledgling attempts to understand the world around her.

Vivica yawned and Sally laughed. "Yes, it's time for my sweetie to take her nap." She picked up her baby and snuggled her to her breast. The tiny, fuzz-covered head bobbed on a wobbly neck, so Sally cupped the back of Vivica's head in her hand and hummed a lullaby in her ear.

She inhaled her daughter's pleasant baby scent and rocked from side to side as she hummed. It was quiet here at the end of the country road. Hardly a sound of civilization intruded, but for the occasional plane droning high overhead. If a car came down the road, it was there to visit her. That was a rare occurrence, since Sam had a busy life of his own and Sally lived a relatively solitary existence. That was all right, she told herself. She had her work and her baby.

Birds chirped in the pines; the breeze made the high boughs crackle and murmur among themselves. The day was warm, fragrant with the scent of rich soil and new grass. From somewhere in the distance, drifting along with the zephyr, came the distinct sweetness of Carolina Jessamine.

Encompassing Sally's small lawn, in the hollows and glens and along the roadside, nature was decked out in a bounty of spring colors. Pink primrose and wild bluebonnets bobbed and nodded next to spectacular masses of purple phlox. Shy, violet baby-blue eyes peeped out from shady nooks amid the piney woods. Spring in Texas was a beautiful, bountiful treasure. Sally couldn't imagine a more lovely place on earth, or a more pleasant way to spend a Sunday afternoon.

Well, maybe there was one, slight change she would make in this idyllic picture. Noah's face burst into her mind's eye, disobediently, as it insisted on doing a thousand times every day. Noah Barrett, her hired husband, stepped in and out of her life for one brief, reality-altering week. He helped bring her precious Vivica into the world. Then, the man she loved quietly and without hope, had gone away as swiftly and unexpectedly as he had come.

Sam returned from vacation last week. He'd dropped by to meet Vivica and to bring Sally chicken in a bucket, a big brother's idea of welcoming a niece into the world. When she'd been unable to keep from asking about Noah, Sam shrugged and said he hadn't seen him or Jane, either on vacation or since they'd returned.

Sally wished she hadn't asked. Did she really need to know Noah and his ladylove had been so busy getting reacquainted he hadn't bothered to go scuba diving with his diving buddy on his scuba diving vacation? The knowledge burned constantly in her heart, no matter how hard she tried to forget.

She held Vivica in her arms and gazed down at her. Tiny, sweet eyelids lolled and closed. Pushing thoughts of Noah to a dark corner of her heart, she kissed her daughter's forehead, gently laying her on the spread and covering her with a light flannel baby blanket. Vivica would take a long afternoon siesta. Now Sally could eat her sandwich, sip her iced tea and read a little before she, too, dozed off to the musical twitter of birds and a summery breeze that hummed through the pines.

Sally's dreams were destroying her rest. Once again Noah's face intruded, the sound of his voice invaded, even his scent stormed the portals of her slumber. *How unfair. How cruel.* Would she never have another whole, uninterrupted night's sleep, or nap in peace, without being haunted by his image, his utterances, his very essence? Must she endure the rest of her life bedeviled

with memories? Though only a figment of her overwrought imagination, Noah Barrett's relentless trespass
wreaked havoc on her mind, her heart and soul.

She reached out in her sleep to fend off his image,
and slapped it away.

"Ouch, hey!"

She frowned, feeling a sting in her hand. Slowly, she
came awake, still experiencing pain in her fingertips. She
opened her eyes, dumbfounded to see something above
her besides blossoming branches of the dogwood.

There was a face. A familiar, handsome face, looking
down at her with a dubious expression.

"Noah?" she asked, as surprised to hear his name
aloud as she was to see his image—with her eyes open.

He lay a palm against his cheek. "Should I be grateful
you didn't know who it was before you hit me?"

She stared, not daring to hope. "What…" She struggled up to her elbows. "I didn't hear you—I thought
you were a…" She swallowed, too confused to make
sense of what was going on. She shook her head, then
focused on him again. Yes, it did *seem* to be Noah.
"What's going on?"

He had been kneeling. As she sat up, he joined her
on the blanket, his expression serious. "I came by because I need to get something off my chest." He shifted
his gaze to the baby and his expression softened. "She's
beautiful." He looked at Sally again, into her eyes. His
were that wonderful mirror-bright blue that filled her
dreams, and she wanted nothing more in the world than
to dive in and happily drown. "You look great," he said
softly. His lips lifted slightly and only for a second before his expression grew serious again.

Her heart went to her throat, and she found it difficult to speak. He'd come back to give her another piece of his mind? She wasn't sure she could endure it. Clearing her throat, she croaked, "What makes you think I want to hear whatever it is you need to get off your chest?"

He leaned on an arm, his fingertips precariously near her leg. For some bizarre reason she couldn't move away. She silently berated her body for being a sniveling traitor.

"You're going to hear me out, whether you like it or not." He looked determined and stern and wonderful. He was tan and fit and seemed more like a buff movie hunk than a doctor. The tan reminded her he'd recently spent much of his time lying on beaches with his girl-friend. She cringed as lewd visions forced their way into her head.

"Look, Sally," he said, drawing her tortured scowl. "You have a huge flaw."

She ground her teeth. *Fine,* this was all she needed. "Thanks, *Doctor,* for your exalted insight, now if you'll—"

"Don't interrupt," he said, his tone and expression so commanding she found herself shutting up and staring. "I haven't known you long, but I feel we've been through enough for me to know what I'm talking about." He leaned forward, invading her space, but for some reason she couldn't back away. Some part of her thrilled at his nearness, cried out with joy, pleaded for his touch, his kiss. She swallowed hard, working to shut out such ludicrous and dangerous thoughts. "Sally," he went on. "You have a bad tendency to hold grudges against people who belittle you."

She was stunned by his audacity. How dare he drive all the way out here to criticize! She bristled, opening her mouth to tell him where he could go with his opinion.

"Don't!" His order was so vehement, so unlike him, she clamped her jaws, answering with a glower. "This grudge-holding is a defense mechanism. You used it against your grandparents for a lot of years. I was glad to see, once you got to know them, you got over it. I was proud of you."

She seethed from the top of her head to the tips of her toes, but the "I was proud of you" comment threw a splash of water on her rage. Never mind; she had plenty of fire left for her scathing response. Just wait until he finished his little correctional speech! She would tell him a thing or two about how much she cared for his I-am-a-doctor-so-my-word-is-law attitude.

"You need to get over your antagonism of doctors," he said, as though he'd read her mind. "Just because one jerk who happened to graduate from medical school made you feel like a second-class citizen, don't blame us all. You have nothing to be ashamed of and you never did. Go ahead and hate jerks if you want to, but give the rest of us a break."

She glared at him, a wave of confusion engulfing her. What was he doing? Somehow the stern correctional speech had turned into very serious, very adamant— *praise.*

She eyed him skeptically, feeling off balance.

"Now you can talk," he said, more gently.

A minute of baffled speechlessness ticked by as birds sang in the trees, oblivious to the tension stretching out between the people far below. "Okay, I—I don't hate you," she said, the edge to her voice more cautious than angry. "Is that all?"

"No," he said, his tone lower, huskier. His gaze captured hers, blue eyes direct and flashing azure fire. Her breath caught at the sight. "No, Sally, it's not." He took her hand, startling her so badly she gasped.

He seemed to wince but the look was brief and might have been the work of Sally's muddled senses. How long had she dreamed of once again knowing even his most casual touch?

His gaze clung to hers, gauging, searching her features. "I'm just going to say this straight out, okay?"

She didn't know what to say, she was so confused. It seemed her brain had been rendered useless by his touch. "O-okay," she whispered.

He squeezed her fingers gently. "Sally, marry me." The brief request brimmed with tenderness and passion. His expression mingled desire and vulnerability. The effect was stunning and she could only stare, as waves of shock ran through her body, zinging and singing and paralyzing with the unbelievable message.

"I love you," he added softly.

Sally thought Noah had a wonderful voice, so deep and clear. But she was having trouble with what his wonderful voice was telling her. It sounded like I love you. Did she dare believe her ears?

"Sally?" He lifted his hands to her shoulders, his touch gentle. "Let me be Vivica's daddy. That night when I delivered her, I—I felt—I knew there would never be any other woman in my life but you. But, I had to go—had to break it off with..."

He let the sentence die and shook his head. "I went off by myself, spent a week walking along the beach, alone, trying to think of ways to tell you, to convince you, to give me a chance to…" Two deep lines of worry appeared between his eyes, as though he was searching for words. He cleared his throat. "Sally, you're what I've been searching for. I need you in my life. I need the peace of losing myself every night in the warmth of an intelligent woman's loving smile. *Your* smile, darling."

He moved closer, brushed her lips with his. "I know you said you don't need a father for Vivica, and I know you're perfectly capable of raising her by yourself. I also know how you feel about doctors." Striking, earnest eyes searched her face. His assurances, his openness and sincerity, sent a tingle of wonder racing through her. "I'm no prize, Sally. You'd have to deal with a husband who could be called into work at all hours, miss dinners and screw up vacation plans, but—"

"Yes," she breathed on a sigh.

Noah stopped, looked puzzled. "What?"

She smiled, wrapped in a silken cocoon of joy. Noah loved her! He wanted to be Vivica's daddy! Heaven had opened its doors and ushered her into paradise. She slid her arms around his sturdy middle and whispered into his ear, "Yes, darling. I will marry you."

Though she hugged him tight, she leaned back enough to look into his face. With a soft kiss on his lips, she murmured, "For the record, I love you. And I happen to be very comfortable with nonconformity."

His eyes caressed softly as his arms encircled her. The feel of him holding her was miraculous and exhilarating.

Her heart sang. For the first time in her life, she felt fully alive and blissfully happy.

She decided she could trust this marvelous man, her one true love, with a secret she'd been keeping from the entire world. "You might as well know. I want three babies before I'm thirty." She took a deep breath and eyed him sheepishly. "If you want to back out, tell me now."

With a sexy chuckle, he gathered her into his lap. "I'll tell you this, sugarplum…" He held her gently, his smile tender, his eyes full of promises she knew in her soul he would keep, and keep well. "If we're going to meet that goal, we haven't a moment to lose."

Even with Noah's hectic schedule, they met Sally's baby deadline. Joining Vivica in quick succession in their lively, loving household, came William and finally Cynthia, arriving on Sally's thirtieth birthday.

As for Abigail and Hubert, they eventually recovered from the amazement of learning their Texas-bred granddaughter had married a Boston Barrett. To this day the Vanderkellens make a point of showing off to house guests the fabulous, wrought-iron banister created by their "brilliant and talented granddaughter."

And the only time the Barretts of Houston make the society pages, these days, is when they visit family in Boston.

Some things never change.

SINGLE IN THE CITY...

English heiresses Annis and Bella are as
different as sisters can be. Annis is clever
and quiet, Bella beautiful and bubbly.
Yet with a millionaire father, they both think
they'll never find a man who wants them
for *themselves*....

How wrong can they be!

Don't miss this fabulous duet by rising star

Sophie Weston

THE MILLIONAIRE'S DAUGHTER
January 2002 #3683

THE BRIDESMAID'S SECRET
February 2002 #3687

in

Harlequin Romance®

HARLEQUIN®
Makes any time special®

Visit us at www.eHarlequin.com   HRWESTON